THE LADY OF THE BOG

GILLIAN ST. KEVERN

To Stripes and Nala,

Thanks for the cuddles!

The front door slammed, rattling the bone china teacups in their saucers. Florence flinched, splashing herself with tea. She bit back a pained hiss, steadying the teapot against the edge of the side table.

"Your father." Mrs Skelton patted her hair to make sure all pins were accounted for. "He'll want a cup of tea."

As Hannah snatched up the thread she'd spread over the best chair, Florence mopped up the spilt tea, conscious of the approaching footsteps. She took the last cup from the tray and turned it right way up.

When Mr Skelton opened the door, it was to a scene of domestic bliss. His wife looked up from her knitting, Hannah's black ringlets bobbed as she bent over her needle-work, and Florence poured his tea.

Mr Skelton had seen the scene so many times he took it for granted. He shut the door behind him with enough force to rattle the landscapes.

"Good afternoon, dear." Mrs Skelton greeted her spouse without surprise. "I hope the choirboys haven't been misbe-having again." She spoke without hope—the natural tone of anyone acquainted with choirboys.

"Little devils," Mr Skelton snarled. He was a broad-shouldered man of medium height and had made a credible scrum half for his college rugby team. He had clever brown eyes, charcoal grey hair and whiskers, and, on the frequent occasions he was angry, red blotches above his clerical collar. "No, it's not the choirboys. My dear Leticia, you must brace yourself. To think my parish would harbour such—such filth!"

Florence dropped a single cube of sugar into her father's teacup as noiselessly as possible. What on earth had occurred? Had one of the village maids lost her virtue? Had a youth been discovered tipsy?

Mrs Skelton pressed her lips together. "If it's the new schoolteacher, I've always said—"

Mr Skelton dropped into his chair. "The reading library. I was under the impression that, although a private enterprise, it would serve our community with works of an edifying, Christian nature. Instead—" He choked on his rage.

"Not sensation novels!" Mrs Skelton held a hand before her mouth. "Or Mr Darwin's book?"

"Worse," Mr Skelton intoned. "Even now, a copy of *Jane Eyre* is circulating in this very parish."

Florence jerked, dropping the sugar tongs.

"Florence!" Mrs Skelton frowned at her eldest daughter.

"Leave her be. Her shock is only natural." Having caused an uproar, Mr Skelton's mood was subsiding. "The pernicious influence of this—this *novel*—is well known." His gaze fell on the teacup Florence held. "Milk, Florence."

Florence plastered a smile on her face and poured the milk. As she did so, she reached out with one foot, drawing her sewing basket beneath her chair where her skirt would screen it. If her father was in this much of a temper because *Jane Eyre* was in his parish, his reaction to learning there was a copy beneath his very roof would be unthinkable.

"Can a book—even a novel—be so bad?" Hannah wondered.

Mr Skelton beamed as he looked at her. "My dear child. There speaks innocence incarnate. To a pure nature like yours, nothing is harm. But to others whose nature is not so good as yours, sinful urges wrapped up in pretty words and romance can have a dire effect."

Hannah fluttered her eyelashes as she cast her gaze downward. Her black hair contrasted against her pink cheeks and rosebud lips: the perfect Victorian doll.

Mr Skelton's gaze passed to his other daughter. A shadow came over his face. Florence knew what he saw when he looked at her—a woman lacking. She possessed neither the pretty femininity of a natural mother, nor the stark self-denial of a saint. Her mousy-brown hair neither curled nor hung straight. She was thin and angular, lacking curves. Stubborn where she should be delicate and weak where she should be strong—unsatisfactory in any family, but in a vicar's family...

She swallowed. She must return *Jane Eyre* to the library before the vicar discovered just where the book was circulating.

"There must be some mistake," Mrs Skelton said. "Haversham has always struck me as a sensible, upright man."

"Haversham is a fool. Too busy with his produce to even read the books he orders. The result of giving the lower classes a bit of education—they presume to know things." Mr Skelton thumped the arm of his chair with the hand not holding his tea. "The current mania for indiscriminate education has a lot to answer for. There is a natural order—"

Florence smiled and nodded. Once he launched on the natural order of things, Mr Skelton could proceed for some time. She concentrated on suppressing the nervous tremble in her hands. When ten minutes had passed, she rose, lifted her sewing basket and faded from the room.

It took all her self-control not to run up the stairs. Alone in her room, Florence took *Jane Eyre* from its hiding place in her sewing basket, bundled it in her plainest shawl and crept downstairs again. The rumbles of her father's voice reached her even through the wall. Still going strong.

Good.

She took a wicker basket from the pantry, placed *Jane Eyre* inside, and covered it with a loaf of bread and a jar of preserves. There was always a parishioner in need of visiting. Throwing the shawl over her head, she snuck out of the house, heart pounding.

She kept a steady pace until the vicarage gate closed behind her. Then, her self-control failed. Florence ran down the country lane. Cutting through the village was faster, but could she risk being seen? Better to take the long route around the village.

Florence rounded a corner, seeing the figure too late to stop. She slammed into the woman at full speed, throwing both of them to the ground. The force of the fall jerked the basket out of her grip.

Florence's vision swam from day to night, then back to day again. "I'm so sorry—so very sorry." She ignored her stinging palms and pounding head and rolled onto her knees. "Are you hurt?"

"Takes more than that to put me out of action." The voice that answered was new to Florence. "You'll have to do better next time."

Next time? Florence stared at her, feeling the sting of a second shock. This woman had all the same basic ingredients as Florence, but the difference between them was as great as that between bread and cake. Her glossy brown hair was speckled through with streaks of grey and warmer sun-tones and was gathered in a careless bun. She stood, dusting herself off. Her plain grey dress with its tightly buttoned-up neck and full skirts would not have looked out of place in Florence's wardrobe either, but she wore it with a grace that Florence would never possess.

She stretched out her hand to Florence with a lack of self-consciousness that indicated she was unaware of her arresting beauty.

Florence, still stunned, took her hand.

The woman looked at her, raising an eyebrow. Wait—had she spoken?

Florence flushed. "I beg your pardon?"

"I said, 'You look like you need to sit down.' There's a stile, just over there." She bent to gather up Florence's scattered belongings.

"I can't." *Jane Eyre*! She had to get the book before— Florence gasped, seeing the offending volume in the other woman's hands. Done for.

"*Jane Eyre?*" The woman turned over the volume, her tone hushed.

Florence swallowed. "I… I can explain."

"I adore Jane!" Her companion hugged the book to her chest. "Her voice—talk about compelling! Her struggles… Nothing's sugar-coated, it's life, just as it is."

Florence stared. Had she hit her head in the fall?

Her companion sighed. "The anguish of her suffering—I couldn't stop reading it."

Florence nodded. "The depth of her feeling—it's like seeing her soul committed to paper."

The woman beamed. "You said it! Her desire for autonomy, for recognition, for self-determination—"

Florence heard the crunch of footsteps too late. Her father rounded the corner. She turned back to her companion, darting her a desperate look. "Please—"

Mr Skelton paused, sizing up the scene. "Florence? I hardly expected—" His eyes fell on the offending volume, still clutched to the woman's chest. He spat his next words. "*Jane Eyre.*"

The woman stiffened. "You have something against this book?"

"Indeed." The vicar held out his hand for it. "I object to anything that excites dangerous notions in women."

Florence could not move. She darted a look at her companion, wishing her far from her father's displeasure.

Two red circles burned in the woman's cheeks. "What *dangerous notions* do you speak of? That a woman feels as much or even more than a man? That she might possess intelligence—want some say in her destiny—that—"

"Enough!" Mr Skelton thundered in the voice that never failed to bring even the rowdiest of choirboys under control. "It is obvious you are already under the book's pernicious influence. Hand it to me–I intend to see it destroyed."

The woman arched an eyebrow. "In that case, I will most certainly not give it to you."

Florence's mouth flew open. The ground cracking open beneath her and plunging her into the bowels of the earth would not have astonished her more. No one defied the vicar.

Mr Skelton gaped. He forced himself to smile, making a slight bow. "Perhaps you do not recognise me. No doubt you are a newcomer to our neighbourhood. I am Horace Skelton, vicar of this parish."

"Rosemary Scott." She lifted her chin in the air. "And I wouldn't give you this book, even if you were the Archbishop of Canterbury."

Florence's head swum. The pounding in her ears made thinking impossible. Was she hallucinating? There could be no other explanation...

Mr Skelton took a step towards Rosemary. "*You—*"

"Father!" Florence grabbed his arm, confused by thoughts

of preventing something dreadful from occurring. "Miss Scott is a newcomer—"

Angry crimson consumed her father's face. He shook Florence's hand from his arm. Then he turned back to Rosemary, pressing his lips together in a ghastly approximation of a smile. "My dear child. You are young, and I grant that I am —as yet—unknown to you. However, I beg that you allow me to guide you. I am a man of the cloth and I have seen much of the world. I know the danger to young minds of such"—his mouth twisted—"*literature*. The only place for this book is the fire."

Rosemary looked him in the face. "Save your sermons for Sunday. You don't know me—and you know even less of my mind. I may choose my reading matter, and I say again: you will not destroy this book."

Mr Skelton squared his shoulders. "This is pure folly! Should you refuse to hand over the book, the outcome is the same. I shall talk to Haversham and make him see the evils he is harbouring. He will agree to destroying the book, of that I have no doubt."

"Indeed?" Rosemary's reply was cool. Did she have blood of ice? "Then I must persuade him to sell it to me. Good day, Vicar—Miss Skelton." With a curt curtsey, she walked off.

Florence watched her stride away, her gait brisk but not hurried.

"Of all the—!" The vicar exploded. "Never have I been so insulted—and in my parish, by a mere slip of a girl!"

"Indeed." Florence stared after Rosemary. How was it possible that she had met the vicar's anger head on and not flinched?

"Who does this Miss Scott think she is?" The vicar scowled after her. "A more dangerous young lady I have never encountered."

"Extraordinary," Florence breathed.

"Whoever she is, I will take her to account. Come,

Florence." The vicar turned towards home. "Your mother must hear of this."

Florence shook herself, bending to gather up her basket and the preserves. Her heart raced, the relief of escaping her father's fury giving way to dread.

Poor Miss Scott. She had no idea what storm she'd unleashed.

2

M rs Skelton's eyes glinted. "Miss Scott is the sister of the tutor Mr Leighton employs for his son. The girl returned from Paris with them and lives at Foxwood Court. No one knows anything about her." She sat in the vicarage sitting room, hands busy with the altarpiece she was embroidering.

"Foxwood Court," Mr Skelton growled. He leaned against the mantelpiece, scowling down at his family. "A young woman in that household... I should have been told."

Florence kept her head bent over her darning, hoping her burning cheeks would not reveal her keen interest in the subject of conversation.

Mrs Skelton pursed her lips. "Miss Scott is not quite... A tutor is a servant, even an educated one. I have not discovered anything about Mr Scott's family. For all we know, his parents could be in trade."

The vicar stroked his mutton chops. "Naturally, I do not consider Miss Scott an equal, Leticia. But it remains our Christian duty to intervene on her behalf."

Florence's heart thudded in her chest. "Do you propose to visit Lord Cross?"

The vicar nodded. "I never shirk my duty." His gaze rested on Florence, busy with her mending, and Hannah, embroidering a handkerchief. "We will go as a family."

"Horace, think of the girls!" Mrs Skelton protested. "Lord Cross keeps a most irregular establishment. He has no housekeeper, as I understand. A bachelor household—and Mr Leighton returned from Paris with a drawing master for his ward."

Mr Skelton's frown deepened. "Don't tell me we have a Frenchman in our midst?"

Mrs Skelton shook her head, biting off the thread she was using. "I should hope not! Mr Dawson is an Englishman and a gentleman."

The vicar snorted. "An artist is no gentleman."

"Perhaps we should be grateful that Mr Leighton brought back a drawing master and not an addition to that awful collection of his," Hannah remarked.

"I will not have Mr Leighton's collection alluded to in this house!" The vicar gave his daughters a warning stare, then turned to his wife. "This conversation has only further convinced me. We cannot let that young woman reside in a house of such ill repute without protest. I must inform Mr Scott of the harm to his sister's reputation that will accrue from so irregular an arrangement."

Mrs Skelton inclined her head. "Still, I think it most unwise. What of the harm to your own daughters' reputations should it become known they have called on such a household?"

"My daughters are above reproach." Mr Skelton surveyed his offspring complacently. "The charitable nature of our errand puts their behaviour outside of criticism, and their upbringing will protect them from any pernicious influences." He nodded, satisfied with his decision. "We shall go tomorrow afternoon."

After lunch the following day, the three women assembled in the sitting room, dressed for visiting. Mrs Skelton wore the brown serge she reserved for parishioners of quality, paired with a plain collar. A maroon shawl and a flower on her bonnet saved her from the suspicion of puritanism.

Mrs Skelton considered Florence, outfitted in her habitual serviceable grey wool. "Can you do nothing to control your hair?"

Florence grimaced, poking the offending strands back under her bonnet.

Hannah smiled at the mirror, adjusting her Sunday bonnet. It was a smart design, copied from the London fashion plates and festooned with the best silk flowers she could fashion.

Her actions caught Mrs Skelton's eye. "Your best bonnet, Hannah? This is not a pleasure call, but a matter of duty."

"True, Mama. But Lord Cross has a wide circle of acquaintances in London, and I would not have him think Father could not afford to outfit his daughters like ladies."

The vicar entered as she spoke. "You will always be recognised as a lady, my dear. Let us go."

Mrs Skelton used the walk to remind her daughters of the behaviour she expected of them. Florence listened with half an ear, much more interested in the wild depths of Foxwood Park. She was not permitted to walk there alone. Breathing in the rich smell of the humus, she felt her chest rise, buoyed by the secret beauty of the wood. If nothing else, at least the walk was pleasant.

At length, she beheld stone arches through the mossy woods. Her heart jolted. In a few minutes, they would stand before the aristocratic bulk of Foxwood Court.

"Now, girls; it is possible that the two of you might find yourselves alone with Miss Scott and Master Westaway." The

Vicar employed the heavy metal knocker on the grand front door. "If so, I trust you know your duty."

"Yes, Papa," Hannah said.

Florence ducked her head. Her heart raced, even more so than it did before she took the village children for Sunday school.

A uniformed footman showed them into the cloakroom. "Lord Cross is entertaining a guest in the library. This way if you please."

Florence darted a surreptitious glance at the paintings they passed but saw nothing outré in the landscapes and still lifes deserving the reputation that Mr Leighton's collection had amassed. She caught herself—of course, such improper objects would not be on public display.

The footman threw open a door into a wood-panelled room. "The Reverend Mr Skelton and family."

Florence inhaled the woody scent of paper with rapture. She gazed at the full bookshelves. Imagine having a library of one's own!

Lord Cross reclined in an armchair before the fire. He stood with a brief bow. "You have excellent timing, vicar. We were just talking about you." He beckoned a second man forward. "My guest was just wondering if you were the same Mr Skelton he knew from Wycliffe."

A blond-haired man stepped forward, eyes sparkling behind his spectacles. "Skelton! This is an unexpected pleasure."

"Temple!" Mr Skelton seized his hand, clapping him on the shoulder. "What brings you to these parts?"

Mr Temple removed his glasses, polishing them on his handkerchief. "I am giving a historical lecture in Rotheram tomorrow afternoon. Lord Cross, knowing something of my work, invited me to stay with him." He nodded to the third man in the library. "Mr Leighton and I have been discussing methods of preserving archaeological finds."

Florence cast a worried look at her father. His brow furrowed. "Archaeological finds?"

"Mr Temple flatters me," Mr Leighton said. "I am but a novice in archaeology." He turned a cheerful smile on their guests. "Mr Temple has been favouring us with a preview of tomorrow's talk. I've learned more about pre-Roman Britain than I ever knew before."

Mr Skelton's shoulders relaxed. "Is that the subject of your talk? I remember seeing a notice posted in the general store."

Florence breathed a sigh of relief. Discussion turned to Mr Temple's chosen field of study—crisis averted. She drifted closer to the nearest bookcase. The leather-bound volumes were a varied bunch, no two the same size. She recognised German, Latin, French, even Greek among the titles. Turning aside, she looked down at a glass-topped display case.

What on earth...?

At first glance it looked like a candle in a candlestick holder, but the cup had a marked resemblance to fingers... Florence stared, her mouth dropping open. Those were fingers! A severed hand, bleached of colour and shrunken, wrapped around a candle...

"A hand of glory. The preserved hand of a hanged man combined with a candle made from the fat of his corpse." Mr Leighton stood beside her. "Not the most savoury of my collection of curiosities. Perhaps I should cover this while your good mother is present." He threw a heavy velvet cover over the case.

Florence blinked, trying to rid her mind of the image. "Why would anyone have such a—a ghastly thing?"

"Superstition," Mr Leighton said, smoothing down the cover. "Some believe that lighting the candle will confer on the bearer a light only they can see, open any door and render motionless any who come within its sphere of light. I have not tested its efficacy out for myself. Lord Cross believes it would have a poor effect on household morale."

Florence transferred her stare to him. Mr Leighton was a man of middle years, chestnut hair swept off his face in a style that had been fashionable a few years since. He was clean shaven, dressed in respectable tweeds, and spoke with the accent of a good university. His expression was wry. It reminded Florence of her Sunday school pupils when she caught them doing something they shouldn't.

"I rarely display it, but our guest was curious." Mr Leighton nodded, motioning Florence towards the rest of their group. "Won't you be more comfortable nearer the fire?"

Florence saw her mother's eyes on her and only then realised her situation: standing to one side with a bachelor—and not just any bachelor, but Mr Leighton of such unusual reputation! "Thank you," she said, regaining the safety of the fold without delay.

"To what do we owe this charming visit?" Something in Lord Cross's manner hinted at impatience.

Mr Skelton coughed. "It is a somewhat delicate errand. Am I correct in thinking there is a young lady resident here?"

Lord Cross's expression was ironic. "Ah, yes. Miss Scott mentioned she had made your acquaintance."

"Then I'm sure a man such as yourself can guess my errand," Mr Skelton bowed. "I am here to offer Mr Scott some advice about his sister."

Lord Cross's eyebrow arched. Mr Leighton shifted. Nervous? Florence felt a weight in the room that had not been there previously.

"What's this about me?" Rosemary stood in the doorway, a defiant lilt to her chin.

3

Florence's mouth parted in a soundless cry. She stared at Rosemary, feeling as though caught in an act of betrayal. If she'd walked into a room to find herself discussed, she would die.

Rosemary did not seem in immediate danger of dying. Her mouth tightened, and she levelled her gaze at the vicar. "Well?" She stood arm in arm with Mr Leighton's son. Julian was a slender boy, whose ashen blond hair was almost white. He watched the group with a wary expression.

Lord Cross inclined his head in their direction. "May I present Miss Rosemary Scott. Miss Scott, you know Mr and Miss Skelton already, but allow me to introduce Mrs Skelton and Miss Hannah."

Mrs Skelton's curtsey was brief, Hannah's flutter of skirts charm personified.

"How do you do." Rosemary gave a brief nod, not taking her eyes off the vicar.

Mrs Skelton's eyes fixed on Rosemary's arm, still resting on Julian's. Her mouth pursed.

Florence's heart sank. Her mother couldn't think there was anything untoward in that gesture, surely? Julian's shyness was obvious. Florence stepped forward, smiling at the boy. "Good afternoon, Julian. Did you enjoy Paris?"

Julian considered her question. "Parts of it I liked. How do you do, Miss Skelton."

"Well, thank you." Florence steeled herself, raising her gaze to Rosemary's. "How do you do."

Rosemary's eyes flashed. "Is no one going to answer my question? If I am the subject of a conversation, you should include me."

Mr Skelton looked down at her. "I am here to speak to your brother."

Rosemary snorted. "Am I mute? I can speak for myself."

"Rosemary," Mr Scott said sotto voce. "Please." He'd also entered the library without anyone noticing. Two coats rested on his arm. Clearly he'd intended to take his charge for a walk. A lean man stood beside him, forehead creased with concern. The artist, Mr Dawson.

Rosemary stared at him. It was as if a door had slammed on her emotions. Blank faced, she walked from the room.

How dreadful. Florence's heart cleaved in her chest. She trembled with nervous energy, nerves at fever pitch. There was going to be a scene. Her mother radiated rigid disapproval; her father projected mingled scorn and fury, and Mr Scott's worry was clear.

"Miss Scott is a very independent young woman," Lord Cross said. "She is still getting settled in to Foxwood. You will excuse her." There was no request in his statement.

"Julian." Mr Leighton looked towards the door.

Julian flinched. "Yes, father?"

"Remember what we talked about?" Mr Leighton prompted. He looked meaningfully towards Hannah and Florence and cocked his head towards the door.

Julian's expression cleared. "Miss Skelton, Miss Hannah, would you care to see the gardens? Apparently they're rather nice."

Hannah's cheeks dimpled. "We'd be delighted."

Florence winced. Hannah's enthusiasm was just as out of place as Rosemary's anger—and just as alarming to Julian. "That is a lovely thought, Julian. Thank you."

He offered her a slight smile and held out his arm.

Florence took it, walking from the room. "Mr Dawson is your drawing instructor? He looks nice."

Julian ducked his head. "He is."

"He's very handsome," Hannah said. "I suppose that comes of living in Paris."

Julian frowned at her. "He's kind to animals. And to me."

Hannah laughed. "An admirable resume!"

Florence frowned at her. Julian was already far too sensitive. They'd met when Mr Leighton had brought his son to assist at the Christmas fete for the poor children of the parish. The children were a cheerful, rambunctious lot, and Florence had greeted the Magic Lantern show with relief. She'd stolen up to her bedroom, intending to snatch a half hour's peace, and discovered Julian curled up on the floor beside her bookcase, paging through her volume of *Moral Tales.* He'd confessed that he found the other children alarming, a sentiment that Florence could relate to. She hadn't convinced him to join the fete, but they'd had an interesting discussion about morals in books.

She cast her mind around for a safe subject. "Are your lessons going well?"

"As well as lessons can go," Julian said.

"What a frightful bore," Hannah replied. "It seems so cruel, having to sit in a stuffy room and read Latin all day."

Florence eyed her sister. Was it only yesterday Hannah had remarked, in the presence of the young schoolmaster, how much she admired learning and how she wished she had a mind that could grasp things like Latin?

Florence's heart pounded—Rosemary paced by the front door. She looked up as they approached, her jaw hardening.

"Are these your cloaks? You'll want them. It can be cold in the woods."

Was the feeling that set Florence's heart racing trepidation or anticipation? "Are you joining us, Miss Scott?"

Rosemary looked at her. "Do you want me to?"

The boldness of the question sent blood rushing to Florence's cheeks. She remembered Lord Cross's words—Rosemary was still settling into Foxwood. "Please."

"Very well." Rosemary threw a cloak over her own shoulders and walked out into the garden.

Hannah exclaimed over the early snowdrops, just coming out on the edge of the woods. "I adore snowdrops. So delicate, don't you think?" She turned to Julian.

Julian stepped back, colliding with Florence. "They are pleasant enough, I suppose."

"Only pleasant? What flower is your favourite, Mr Westaway?" Hannah's tone was playful.

Julian cast a desperate look at Rosemary.

She put a hand on his shoulder. "Miss Hannah would like you to show her the flowers. Offer her your arm, like a good gentleman."

Julian proffered his arm. "Care to see the flowers, Miss Hannah?"

Hannah giggled, taking it. "I thought you'd never ask."

"Miss Hannah is a very pretty girl," Rosemary continued. "You mustn't talk only about the flowers. Compliment her and find out what her interests are." She turned to Hannah. "Go easy on him. There's not much chance to practice flirting at Foxwood Court. Julian is very much a novice."

Hannah's laugh was forced, but Julian took his instructions with apparent seriousness. "If you like snowdrops, there are more of them by the lake."

Hannah was willing. The two of them walked off, Hannah's light prattle punctuated by occasional remarks from Julian.

"Keep a tight grip on his arm!" Rosemary yelled after them. "He's liable to escape." She watched them go, a rueful look on her face. "The experience will be good for him. He will be an extremely eligible bachelor someday."

"He's safe with Hannah," Florence said. "She flirts with everyone, but she always remains within the bounds of good behaviour."

"Indeed." Rosemary's tone was ironic. "I daresay your father keeps her within bounds."

Florence's shoulders drooped. "It is on that subject that we are here," her voice wobbled. "Father's object in visiting today is to acquaint your brother with your choice of reading matter."

"Basil's already aware that I read *Jane Eyre*. I borrowed three shillings off him to buy the book."

Three shillings! What an inordinate sum! "Was he furious?"

"No. If anything he was pleased to do something for me." Rosemary's tone was scornful. "He urged me to think of it as a gift, but I will pay him back next quarter when I get my salary."

Florence glanced around, checking that Hannah wasn't in earshot. "You—work?"

"Cataloguing the library and acting as a companion to Julian. I intend to find a proper job once my education is complete." Again there was that odd note in Rosemary's voice.

Florence let Rosemary lead her towards the gazebo perched atop the rise looking down at the lake. "You don't want to remain here?"

"In Foxwood? I'd suffocate."

Florence looked to the house. Her eyes travelled over the park, the gardens, contrasting them against the small confines of the vicarage and the grey stone wall surrounding the graveyard. "Suffocated... here?"

Rosemary let go of her arm, walking to far end of the gazebo. "Lord Cross has been very generous. Mr Leighton, too. That's the problem." She turned back to face Florence, lifting her chin, shoulders squared for an argument. "I can't be independent living on charity. I must live life on my terms, owing nothing to anyone."

Florence stretched out a hand to steady herself against the gazebo posts. Admiration surged in her breast even as her knees felt weak with fear. "But your reputation! A lady living without a protector—"

"I'm not a lady." Rosemary squared her shoulders. "I'm from good, honest farming stock, and not ashamed to say so." She held up weathered hands. "These hands have swept floors, milked cows, churned butter—and more—much more."

Florence stepped forward, putting her hand atop Rosemary's. Rough, yes, but warm and strong. How had she wound up in the world of Foxwood Court? "Your marriage prospects. A woman's reputation—"

Rosemary's hand clenched beneath Florence's touch. "I cannot contemplate marriage in our present society. Without equality, what union would be bearable?"

Florence swallowed. She had heard her father hold forth on the natural place of women many times. She could quote by heart all the bible passages to support women as help-meet. Before Rosemary's simple statement, they all fell short. "Won't you be lonely?"

Rosemary inclined her head. "If that is the price of freedom, then I shall pay it." She looked up, spearing Florence with her bright, hard gaze. "And you?"

Florence caught her breath. "Me?"

Rosemary arched an eyebrow at her. "You can't want to spend the rest of your life as the vicar's daughter."

Want, no. But since when had Florence's wants mattered? "There's nothing else I can do."

"Marriage?"

Florence fought the urge to further disorder her hair by tugging at it. She blushed because of the direct nature of the question. Not for any other reason. "There's no one in Foxwood that I could marry. And besides—" Florence gathered all her courage and made the plunge. "I don't think I am suited to matrimony."

Anyone else would have ridiculed that statement. What did a mere girl know of matrimony? Who was she to deride God's intention for womankind?

Rosemary nodded. "Are you educated?"

"Partly." Florence's cheeks burned. Now she was for it. "My godmother paid for me to go to a school for girls, but I disgraced my family and they withdrew me."

Rosemary whistled. "What did you do? Voice an opinion of your own?"

"I—" Florence dropped Rosemary's gaze. She couldn't bear the sight of the disgust she knew must follow. "My teacher set a composition. I invented a—a story." She pressed her trembling palms against her skirts. "The teacher singled it out for praise and had it published."

"And?" Rosemary waited.

Florence darted a look at her. "Father was furious. To have his daughter author a work of fiction and then to have her name attached to it—it was as bad as if I'd said he was encouraging people to lie."

Rosemary stared at her. "He pulled you out of school for that?"

Florence frowned. This wasn't how she'd seen this conversation going. "The teachers encouraged me. None of them saw anything wrong in what I'd done. They thought I had talent."

"Unforgivable." Rosemary clenched her fists. "How dare they encourage you to have self-respect."

Florence studied Rosemary with dismay. Her tone was

ironic, but how to read her gesture? The conversation had entirely escaped her. How was she supposed to attend to Miss Scott's morals now? "It is hard, but I know this is part of God's plan for me." She tucked a stray wisp of hair behind one ear. "If I'd been at school, I would never have read *Jane Eyre*…or met you."

"One of those things would have been a loss." Rosemary's tone was ironic.

"I mean it." Florence's mouth felt dry. "This conversation we've had this morning—I've never told another soul what I've told you."

"Looks like the conversation is at an end." Rosemary's jaw tightened. "Your father is heading this way. He does not look pleased."

Florence looked up. Her father strode towards them, his shoulders set. "I'd better go." She held out her hand to Miss Scott. "It was nice to meet you."

Rosemary tilted her head to the side. "You sound as though you're saying goodbye."

Florence bowed her head. "I'm very much afraid I might be."

"A most anti-Christian establishment." Mr Skelton sank into his favourite armchair with a sombre air. "Mr Scott is not only cognisant of his sister's dangerous behaviour but tolerates it."

Mrs Skelton shook her head, her needle darting back and forth across her fabric. "I expected nothing less from that household. Lord Cross encourages the village people to become Chartists. He has no regard for the natural order of things. No wonder his household has produced such a—a harridan."

"She isn't—" Florence stopped herself. Arguing with her parents never ended well.

No one heard her, anyway.

"Is it fair to blame Miss Scott on Lord Cross?" Hannah wondered. "Julian told me she's only been residing with them a fortnight."

Mrs Skelton's sniff was expressive. "I wonder at Mr Leighton allowing his ward to fraternise with so unprincipled a young woman. The liberties she takes with him! It's not decent."

Florence's head snapped up. "There's nothing improper

in Miss Scott's relationship to Mr Julian. She treats him like a sibling."

"Most unwise." Mrs Skelton shook her head. "Apart from the difference in age, sex and social status, there is Mr Westaway's wealth. A youthful misalliance could destroy any chances he has of making a name for himself. That is, if his guardian's poor decisions have not already ruined his chances in society."

"I'm sure—" Florence started.

"Be guided by your mother," Mr Skelton said. "No, there shall be no repeat visit to Foxwood Court."

Susan, their sullen housemaid, flung open the sitting-room door. "A Mr Scott to see you." She stepped back, revealing Mr Scott's plump form and sunny expression.

Florence lurched to her feet, her cheeks hot. Had he overheard their conversation? She fumbled her greeting, her mind reliving the last few minutes' conversation.

"Excuse my intrusion." Scott beamed at them. "I am here on an important errand." He bowed to the vicar. "Mr Temple is delighted to find an acquaintance among our neighbours and has sent me with four tickets to his lecture tomorrow."

The vicar didn't stand. "How thoughtful of Mr Temple." His manner was stiff. Mr Scott might let bygones be bygones, but the Vicar made no such choice.

Mr Scott seemed unaware of anything unusual in the vicar's manner. "Since the lectures are in Rotheram, Lord Cross also offers the use of his carriage to transport yourself and those members of your family who would like to attend."

The vicar swallowed with difficulty. "Lord Cross is kind. I had intended to attend the lecture but was wondering how to make the journey."

"Then you accept?" Mr Scott looked eager.

The vicar bowed his head. "I do."

"If the carriage comes by at two, would that suit?" They pinned down the finer details of the arrangements. Mr Scott turned his generous smile on Florence. "Much obliged to you, Miss Skelton, for making my sister welcome in Foxwood."

Florence darted a quick glance at her parents. What would they think? "You are too kind. I did nothing at all."

"It may be nothing to you, but it means an awful lot to me." Mr Scott's expression was hopeful. "Rosemary doesn't complain, but I'm sure she finds it very dull amongst all us men. A friend her own age could be just what she needs. She is, as I'm sure you've noticed, unused to moving in polite society. An exemplar like yourself would benefit her a great deal, Miss Skelton."

Florence stared at the floor, struggling to keep her composure. "You praise me too highly. My conduct is more worthy of your censure than your regard."

"Your modesty is but one of the qualities I hope you will impart to my sister." Mr Scott gave the vicar a nod, bowed to Mrs Skelton and Hannah, and took his leave.

Florence sank back into her seat with relief.

The ordeal was over!

Mrs Skelton resumed her seat with a pointed sniff. "I wonder at you, Horace! If we are not to call on Foxwood Court, surely accepting the offer of Lord Cross's carriage is just as improper?"

"An excellent point, Leticia." Mr Skelton resumed his seat. "And one I had considered. However, it is likely that Lord Cross's kind gesture is not directed at us but at Mr Temple, his guest. We can accept it with no suggestion of intimacy between our households. It is unlikely that Lord Cross intends to ride with us."

Mrs Skelton bowed her head. "You are correct." She glanced at Florence. "I daresay that Miss Scott will be attending this lecture."

"What is the lecture, father?" Florence asked. If she could

keep them off the subject of Miss Scott, they might forget to forbid her to go.

"Temple is conducting an archaeological examination of the Aylesport fens. He will present his finds and explain their significance for our understanding of pre-Roman Britain."

"Is it wise to dwell on the lives of a bunch of heathen savages?" Mrs Skelton wondered. "The Romans introduced Christianity and civilisation to these lands."

"Temple has some notion that the Celts had a certain amount of civilisation already," Mr Skelton said. "If that is true, then it would counter any suggestion that this nation of ours would be nothing without the achievements of the Romans."

Mrs Skelton drew her lips together. "I can't consider it a wholesome occupation. How are you acquainted with Mr Temple?"

"We studied together at University. He was a keen historian but had put his natural interests aside and was working towards his priesthood. They ordained us the same month. Temple took a living in Aylesport, where he developed an interest in the archaeology of the area and made the finds that enabled him to resign from the church and pursue his interests as a historian."

Mrs Skelton's eyes rested on Florence. "Is Mr Temple a bachelor?"

The vicar shook his head. "He is married to an Aylesport woman—the woman upon whose land he made his discoveries."

Mrs Skelton tutted. "That's one way to keep it in the family."

"She is not a village woman, Leticia, but a lady."

Mrs Skelton made no immediate reply. After some time, she said, "I wonder Horace, if you intend to take both your daughters to Rotheram? They are not used to such exertion and exposing a young woman to mental effort is liable to have a detrimental effect on her appearance." She placed a hand on Hannah's ringlets. "We cannot risk blighting their looks—or their chances of marriage."

"I don't think one lecture all that much of a risk," Mr Skelton protested. "Still, Hannah is young..."

Florence held her breath. Did she dare hope...?

"You would take Florence then?"

"Temple made his invitation to all of us. It would not look good should I arrive alone. Besides, Florence has no bloom to lose."

Florence kept her gaze focused on her mending, trying to quash the ache that stabbed through her at his words. She was well aware of her plainness. "I should be glad to attend. Mr Temple is kind to invite us."

Mrs Skelton sighed. "We should never have agreed to your education."

"Great Aunt Florence insisted," Mr Skelton reminded her. "And she gave us reason to expect that should Florence perform well, she might have expectations."

"Instead she has taken up with some blue-stocking society. What do they call themselves?"

"The lepidopterist collective." Mr Skelton took his book of sermons from the incidental table and thumbed through it to his desired page.

Mrs Skelton stood, arranging the ornaments on the mantelpiece. "Indeed! And what is a lepidopterist when it is at home?"

"Someone with a particular interest in the study of butterflies and moths," Florence caught herself a moment too late. Had she betrayed her interest in Great-Aunt Florence's doings?

"Butterflies and moths." Mrs Skelton eyed the knick-knacks with dissatisfaction. "A most unladylike interest."

"If I am to accompany father tomorrow, may I be

excused?" Florence asked. "I should like to make sure I am rested."

With permission granted, Florence retreated to her bedroom. She took her best dress from her wardrobe. The rose crepe would do. It was clean and well mended. She set it back and took down her hat. The silk flowers had gathered dust. No one noticed in the dim light of the church, but there was a risk the lecture hall might be better lit. Florence wiped the flowers, petal by petal.

A drumming noise drew her attention to the window. Rain pelted the glass pane. Florence leaped to her feet, pulling the curtains shut.

As she did, she caught a snatch of sound. A voice pitched high and wavering.

Florence heaved the window upright. "Hello?"

The sound of the rain striking the stone walls of the vicarage was the only reply.

Florence hesitated. That had sounded very much like a voice raised in song, or an animal calling…

"Who would sing on a night like this?" Florence closed the window and pulled the curtains shut, muting the rain. She picked up her hat. Nothing but imagination.

5

The rain continued the next day, a persistent grey drizzle that permeated the entire world with gloom. Florence had no time to appreciate the four matched horses or the polished wood of Lord Cross's carriage. She scrambled up into the carriage, hand raised to shield her hat from the rain.

Her father followed on her heels, and with no delay they were off. Once she'd determined the silk flowers of her bonnet were only slightly damp, Florence looked out of the window. They sped past the fields she passed when walking. "Funny how even a slight change in height can make the most familiar sights seem strange."

Her father smiled. "A change in perspective."

Rotheram's principal claim to township was the fact that it possessed a railway station and the town hall where the lecture would take place. Florence found Rotheram's attractions even less imposing viewed from Lord Cross's carriage. "I wonder Mr Temple did not give his talk at Foxwood. Our church hall would have done just as well."

"Proximity to the railway line, no doubt." Mr Skelton assisted his daughter from the carriage. "Temple must hope for a larger audience than he could gather in Foxwood alone. Quickly now."

The footmen ushered them inside with umbrellas. In no time at all, Florence was fixing her bonnet in place, as Mr Temple advanced on her father with a pleased expression. "Skelton, I am delighted you've come."

"I would not miss it." Mr Skelton shook his hand. "Florence and I both look forward to your talk."

Mr Temple inclined his head to Florence. "So delighted you could join us, Miss Skelton. Have you an interest in Britain's history?"

Florence curtsied. "An interest, yes. As to actual knowledge, I must confess I know little. In school, we studied little more than Mary, Elizabeth, and the princes in the tower."

Mr Temple removed his glasses, polishing them again on his handkerchief. "I cannot blame teachers for travelling the well-trodden path. Young minds cannot long focus, and the larger-than-life figures of the tragic Queen of Scots, Richard III or good Queen Bess are topics that even the worst teacher could not make dull—though old Woodrow tried, didn't he, Skelton?"

Her father rumbled. Florence, startled, realised he was laughing. "Poor Woodrow! I have never met a man with a more remarkable talent for making the most interesting subject dull—unless it was Bishop Halifax."

Temple smiled, casting a quick look around the hall. "We ragged him rather hard, didn't we? Still, he is no doubt having his revenge. Halifax never had so poor a showing as this."

Florence glanced around the hall. A handful of people stood talking in the aisles or sat in the rows of chairs. Mr Leighton was busy on stage making sure that the lectern was centred, and Mr Temple provided with a glass of water. There was no sign of the rest of the Foxwood Court party.

Disappointment flooded through Florence. She caught

herself—attending the lecture at all was a great boon. Wishing for more than that was ingratitude in the extreme.

"Nonsense," Mr Skelton said at once. "For these parts, this is a good showing."

Mr Temple shook his head. "This is far from the smallest audience I have spoken to before. It is a shame, as my subject is one that would repay interest if only it were better known! If our countrymen were but better acquainted with their noble ancestry, their pride in themselves would enable them to resist the degenerating influences of the modern world."

"You see your work then as not only educating man but bettering his spiritual condition?" Mr Skelton asked.

Mr Temple squeezed his hand. "I knew you would understand! Any education that does not take the soul of a man into account is incomplete. By looking to the achievements of those who ploughed these very fields in time out of memory, before the Romans—and indeed, who resisted the Romans—we stake our claim to a dynasty equal to that of any other civilisation." He deflated. "But without a gruesome murder or impressive monument such as the Tower of London, I cannot induce the average man to care about so distant a past."

"I have found people reluctant to listen to what will benefit them," Mr Skelton agreed. "My sermons—"

Florence had heard her father complain about the inattention his sermons received many times before. She let her gaze drift around the room. Her eyes met a cold stare fixed on her.

Florence was too surprised not to stare back.

The woman stood alone near the back of the hall. Florence did not recognise her as one of her father's parishioners. She was a few years older than Florence, dressed plainly but respectably in garments that had come off the worst with the weather. Her black hair stuck to her neck in thick tendrils. She did not seem to have a male escort with her—indeed, no escort at all. None of the other people in the hall glanced her way or acknowledged her, nor she them. Yet, she stared at their group.

Who did she watch? Florence stepped aside. The woman's gaze remained resting on her father talking to Mr Temple.

Did she seek the vicar's aid? Florence approached the woman. She could enquire as to the woman's situation and then get her father's attention.

Just before Florence reached the woman, she turned, walking out the door.

Florence followed. Had the woman guessed her intention? Perhaps she was mistaken. It would not look well for Florence to walk alone in the street. She would go as far as the doorway, and if she did not see—

Her foot skidded on the wooden floor of the hall. Florence went down in a heap of petticoats.

"Are you all right, Miss?" A man she did not know approached.

Florence, cheeks flaming, shook her head, refusing the hand he offered. "Thank you, but I am fine." She took a deep breath and levered herself upright using a nearby chair.

Her fall had not gone unnoticed. Her father and Mr Temple approached.

"Are you all right, Miss Skelton?"

"Quite. I merely slipped." Florence smoothed her skirts down, discovering that they were damp. "There is a puddle here."

"So there is." Mr Temple frowned. "We must get that mopped up."

Mr Skelton frowned at his daughter. "I am ashamed of you, making a spectacle of yourself and me. What possessed you to leave my company?"

"There was a woman watching us. I thought perhaps she needed counsel, so I approached her."

Mr Temple tensed, turning back to Florence. "A woman? Can you describe her?"

"She was a little older than me, with black hair, wearing a brown dress, and no hat. Her hair was loose. I do not recall seeing her before."

"Black hair." Mr Temple scanned the room. "She is not here now?" His skin was pale, his voice pitched high.

"No—she left as I drew near." Florence paused. Mr Temple's previous calm had deserted him. "Do you know her?"

"Know her?" Mr Temple repeated, looking towards the door. "No. It is impossible...and yet..." He rubbed his chin. "Black hair, you say? And no hat?" He strode to the door.

Mr Skelton surveyed his daughter. "I do not know what I am to do with you. Councillor Wigram has just stepped through the door—and there is Vicar Pennywise."

Florence made another attempt to smooth down her skirts. "Perhaps if I sit at the back, my skirts will not be so noticeable."

The vicar nodded. "Indeed. I do not want to see any further instances of you making yourself remarkable." He approached the Councillor with a bow.

Florence took a seat in the very back of the hall. More people were arriving now, the seats about half full. Mr Temple must be pleased with that.

She spread her skirts around her, hoping they would dry faster. The damp had penetrated to the petticoats beneath, making for an uncomfortable chill. Just how much water had been spilt?

Mr Temple returned to the podium. He glanced around the hall, barely looking at Mr Leighton who spoke to him.

A sudden bustle of movement drew Florence's attention back to her surroundings as a body squeezed past her. "I'm sorry, am I in your way? I can move—"

"Stay where you are, rabbit." Rosemary plopped down

into the seat beside her. "We've come to sit with you." Mr Scott took the seat on Florence's other side, Julian and the tall, angular man with the impressive set of whiskers taking the seats to his left. The gentlemen raised their hats.

"How pleasant to see you here, Miss Skelton." Mr Scott said. "I trust you're well?"

Florence did not dare look at her father to see if he'd noticed. "Very well."

"We cut it very fine," Mr Dawson observed. "He's starting."

As the gaslight dimmed, Mr Leighton stepped up to the podium. "Ladies and Gentlemen, thank you for braving the weather to join us this afternoon. It gives me great honour to introduce to you a man whose work is well known to those with an interest in the history of our nation, Mr Ignatius Temple."

Florence joined in the round of polite applause but did not return her hand to her lap. Greatly daring, she reached out to find Rosemary's hand. Warm fingers gripped her own.

Florence kept her eyes fixed on the stage, but her heart soared. To be sitting next to Rosemary—actually holding her hand! Not even her father's disapproval could take away her joy.

6

M r Temple spoke well. He delivered his talk with the energy of an enthusiast, bringing Ancient Briton to life, not just with his words, but with the artefacts he displayed and even a few photographs.

"My wife humoured me by agreeing to wear the jewellery we found as the ancient inhabitants of the fens would wear it. I think you will agree with me that she wears them well." The magic lantern projected an image of a dark-haired woman of astonishing beauty, wearing a rough wooden cloak over a tunic. Her hair shone in an elaborate series of plaits and the necklace, coronet, and armbands complimented her regal beauty. She held a rose in one hand. The other rested on the hilt of a sword.

An appreciative murmur arose from the room.

"Notice, if you will, the sword." Mr Temple motioned to the weapon. "Boudica was not the only warrior queen of her time. In amongst jewellery and feminine ornaments, I uncovered weapons—and weapons of a size and delicacy suggesting that not only were they borne by a woman but designed for her. Observe."

A photograph displaying the remains of a rusty sword

next to a wooden replica replaced the lantern slide of Mrs Temple.

"Our ancestors not only respected women but revered them. They attributed the form of a goddess to the nature spirts they worshipped and respected and loved their queens. These artefacts represent the burial of a woman of considerable rank and power, and, judging by the weaponry I have recovered from the site, a woman of no small military achievements. Many of the weapons interred with her showed the mark of battle." Mr Temple turned back to his audience. "It is my belief that the role women played in our ancestors' society was much more active than that we see today—a fact greatly to our detriment."

"Well said," Rosemary murmured. "These present constraints are unnatural."

Florence glanced at her. Rosemary watched the slides with avid attention. It was easy to imagine her in the guise of a warrior queen of old. Her energy would fit her well to command forces and rally troops. But in modern times… Florence's smile faded. What was a suitable channel for energy such as Rosemary's in modern society?

This consideration troubled her throughout the rest of the lecture. She remained seated, deep in thought, long after Mr Temple had finished, listening to Rosemary and her brother discuss their impressions and quiz Julian on his thoughts.

"Congratulations, Mr Temple." Mr Scott shook his hand as he approached the group. "You have done yourself proud. A most interesting lecture!"

Mr Temple nodded, polishing his glasses. "I was fortunate to have so attentive an audience. I am most glad you could make it."

Mr Skelton nodded in greeting to Mr Scott and the rest of the Foxwood Court party. He pretended not to notice

Rosemary, but Florence saw him frown. She stood, taking her place beside him.

"I have not given Ancient Britain much thought before. Your account of your discoveries makes me eager to learn more of the past," Mr Scott said.

"I am pleased to hear so," Mr Temple said. "It is a source of great disappointment to me that more do not know about so rich a period of history. I suppose it is natural—human imagination is drawn to big finds. The treasure of Solomon, the skeletons of the princes. A few pieces of weaponry—no matter how great their impact on our understanding of our past—will not generate the same attention."

Mr Leighton nodded. "You must tell us more over dinner."

"Delighted—but it must be tomorrow." Mr Temple nodded in Mr Skelton's direction. "Mr Skelton has invited me to join him and his family for their evening meal, that we might continue our discussion. I hope you will not mind if I accept his invitation?"

"Of course not," Mr Leighton said. "It is not every day one sees an old friend."

"I am obliged to you," Mr Skelton said. "Please let Lord Cross know how much we appreciated the carriage."

Florence added her thanks to her father's, and after some small talk, a footman let them know the carriage was waiting. In short order, Florence, Mr Skelton, and Mr Temple were making their way back to Foxwood.

"A good talk," Mr Skelton said to Mr Temple. "But I am not sure it was a wise one. There were young women in the audience, and their minds are more easily influenced than those of adults. Your statements about the place of women in ancient society may do great harm."

"By encouraging them to practice more independence? I do not think we have anything to fear from young women lifting some responsibility for their care from the shoulders of those around them." Mr Temple leaned forward. "Helplessness is neither a virtue nor an accomplishment."

"A woman does not have the same capabilities or understanding as a man." Mr Skelton started.

Mr Temple waved a finger at him. "She is not given his education nor the opportunity to gain understanding. I am sure that there are cases in your parish of widows or spinsters who must take on the responsibility of a man and do so well."

Mr Skelton rubbed his chin. "I do not think you'll find that those women would prefer to remain in so precarious a position."

"No doubt you are correct. But is it not better to prepare women for such times, rather than trust them to their male relatives?"

"How do you propose to do that, without also inciting discontent amongst those women whose place is within their family home?"

"Why, by allowing women their own property and letting them dispose of it as they would." Mr Temple nodded to Florence. "I am sure Miss Skelton agrees that to have an income of her own would be no unpleasant thing."

"You will not find many who will argue with you on that point," Florence agreed. "But how may a woman obtain such an income?"

"Where possible, an allowance is no bad thing. A young lady might learn much from being allowed to administer the household budget for a month. And then there is the prospect of her earning."

Mr Skelton coughed. "I did not think I should hear you propose such a course, Ignatius!"

"With reservations. I do not propose to see a female doctor or lawyer, but the role of a governess or a companion could only be undertaken by a woman with the class and integrity of a lady." He nodded to Florence. "I am searching for a young woman to act in the double capacity of secretary to me and companion to my wife. She must have both education, a pleasing personality, and integrity—qualities not often fostered in our young women."

Florence's heart thumped in her chest. Ever since her conversation with Rosemary, the thought of an occupation had been on her mind. Dare she ask more? "Do—"

"I am curious how you have managed your excavations," Mr Skelton said, changing the subject. "The fens must pose unique challenges."

"They do." Mr Temple took the hint, and the conversation switched to archaeological matters.

Much to her dismay, Florence did not get the chance to approach Mr Temple. Upon their arrival home, her mother recruited her to help in the kitchen. The vicarage was well used to accommodating unexpected guests. An extra side dish, Florence's treacle pudding, and the roast contrived to serve five. After dinner, the gentlemen retired to the vicar's study, and the women sewed in the sitting room.

Hannah questioned Florence about the clothes worn by the women at the lecture, and Mrs Skelton on whether any of her acquaintance were present. Before Florence could think of an excuse to enter the study, Mr Temple took his leave.

"I cannot neglect my hosts too long. A pleasure to meet all of you." He bowed low. "Please call on us should you ever be in the vicinity of Aylesport."

"How pleasant to see Temple again." Mr Skelton took his usual seat. "A pity his enthusiasm for his subject has coloured his conclusions."

Mrs Skelton rang for the tea things. "That is the danger of enthusiasm."

Susan set the tea tray down before Florence and made a half-hearted curtsey. Florence picked up the teapot, gathering her courage. "Father, I was thinking about some comments Mr Temple made. Do you think... I could get a job?"

Dead silence.

Florence swallowed. "Something suitable. Companion or governess—"

Mr Skelton stood. "No daughter of mine will ever demean her family by seeking employment. The very idea!"

"Is that what comes of attending a lecture?" Mrs Skelton snapped. "I am ashamed, Florence."

"I am an adult," Florence protested. "Father provides all for my care. Is it not right that I should take some of that responsibility?"

"The duty of a Christian woman is not to think, it is to obey." The vicar picked up the candleholder beside his chair and grabbed Florence by her arm. "You must contemplate the difference in the attic." Mr Skelton pulled his daughter up the stairs and thrust her into the cold, dark attic. "When I return, I trust that I will find that you have meditated on the proper role of a Christian woman."

Florence said nothing. Fury beat in her veins.

Mr Skelton pressed his lips together into a grim line as he considered his daughter. "There is nothing less attractive in a woman than wilfulness." He pulled the door shut behind him, and Florence heard the click of the key turning in the lock.

Alone in the dark, Florence's meagre courage failed her. She sank to her knees. Locked in the attic with the rats—was this to be the rest of her life? Meek obedience or the attic? Hot tears ran down her cheeks. Florence could resist no longer. She sobbed.

7

"I blame literature." Mrs Skelton thumped Florence's cup of tea down on the table. "We should never have allowed her to read *Pride and Prejudice*. In my day we considered a curate a catch. You would not have seen a girl of my generation turn her nose up at a curate!"

Florence did not look up from her bowl of porridge. Her parents had continued to debate her behaviour after they had retired to bed. She couldn't hear the words, but that their anger had not abated was very clear. "Father, I could not in good conscience have accepted Mr Ashley's suit. I would not have made him a worthy wife."

"You cannot afford to be too fastidious," Mr Skelton observed. "You are not likely to receive many proposals." He turned to his wife. "We have not had Mr Ashley to dinner for some time."

"I thought it better not to remind him of Florence's inconsiderate rejection."

"Invite him this Sunday. I am sure that upon reflection he will see that too hasty acceptance is as bad as a rejection and he will respect Florence more for wanting to be sure of her choice."

The porridge stuck in Florence's throat. There was no point in protesting. It would only lead to another stint in the attic. She was so tired. She'd dug an old cloak out of a trunk and made herself passably warm, but had not slept, too aware of the scratching of the mice—or worse—in the rafters. In the small hours of the morning, something had run over her legs. There was no chance of relaxation after that.

She swallowed the scalding tea and stood. "I shall help Susan in the kitchen."

Susan had complaints of her own—too busy with her grievances against her mistress to care for Florence's difficulties. Florence nodded, murmured at intervals, and busied herself with the washing up. Was this all life offered? Domestic duties or the attic?

After lunch she presented herself and her basket. "I thought I'd take some bread and preserves to Old Mrs Williams."

Her mother sniffed. "By rights you shouldn't be going out at all. The way you've behaved…! Still, you are looking rather peaky. You need the fresh air. We can't have you getting sick before Sunday."

Florence trudged down the lane. The countryside, usually a source of relief from the strict rules of the vicarage, was today oppressive. The overcast sky seemed an extension of the grey stone walls of the vicarage, and the lanes were bare of people. Even the flowers drooped, weighed down by the rain that had fallen for much of the night.

Old Mrs Williams, better known as Biddy Williams, lived in a cottage on the very edge of the old forest, the part not contained within Foxwood Park. Smoke curled from the chimney, and early daffodils bloomed in the garden.

Florence felt cheered at the sight. She unhitched Biddy's gate with the first feeling of lightness she'd had all day.

Biddy had the jug already boiling on the fire and the tea

things set out when Florence arrived. "An ill-wind blowing today, Miss Florence."

How was it that Biddy always knew when she had company coming? A thick yew hedge screened her cottage from the road. "Yes. I was very glad of my cloak walking here."

"I don't speak of the cold." Biddy pulled her chair closer to the table. "There's a trial in front of you. The path is murky, easily lost—and yet the journey is worth taking. It will change you."

Biddy's cottage was cosy, but Florence felt a chill. "A trial?" The village grapevine was fast, but Susan could not have broadcast Florence's disgrace so soon.

"It was the tea leaves that told me—not anyone from the village." Biddy picked up her cup of tea, blowing away the steam. Her eyes glinted at Florence from the other side of the cup. "I saw a death."

Despite her father's many admonishments against giving village superstitions any weight, Florence's skin prickled. "You must be mistaken."

"A death," Biddy repeated. "And many things beside. You must prepare to bury Florence Skelton."

Florence shivered. The villagers revered Biddy as a witch, and her father decried her as a pestilent survival of medieval superstition. Florence knew her just as a lonely old woman who compensated for her lack of family with pretend. But for the first time, she heard in Biddy's prediction a ring of something not easily dismissed. "You mustn't scare me."

"Scare? No." Biddy stared into her cup of tea. "Prepare you. There's more in you than you know." She lapsed into silence, staring hard into her teacup.

Florence took her leave with relief. She hastened back down the lane, eager to regain the predictable safety of the vicarage. Biddy's warning had imparted something strange to the familiar landscape. The trees stood stark against the grey clouds, thin branches grasping. The silence that hung over the empty landscape felt remorseless.

Florence turned the corner. The wind slapped her cold in the face, but it was the sight that took her breath away. A woman, stark in outline as the trees, stood up to her knees in the pond.

In the summer that Skelton had first taken over as vicar, a village maid had drowned herself in the pond. For a moment, Florence thought she had returned.

Really, Florence! Be sensible.

She ran, climbing over the stile into the field. The woman obviously needed aid. No one would stand in a pond in late-winter unless—fear clutched her throat—unless she contemplated something dreadful.

"May I be of service?"

The woman turned her brown eyes and sullen stare on Florence. Her black hair hung in sodden ringlets; her dress clung to her thin form.

The woman from the lecture! Florence stared. What was she doing in Foxwood?

"Florence Skelton?" The woman's voice was bitter.

"I am she." Florence stepped closer. "Do you seek the vicar?" No doubt the woman was in the usual difficulty. Was the father a member of the Foxwood parish? "Come to the vicarage. You can warm yourself by the fire while I let my father know you're here."

"I seek you." The woman beckoned Florence closer. "You are young, as I was. Friendless, as I was."

Florence caught her breath, halting on the water's edge. "Wh-who are you to speak to me so?" This was no village maid. Her clothes suggested limited means, but her accents were that of a lady.

"I am your future." The pond rippled as she stepped forward, grasping Florence's hands in her own. Her skin chilled. Pondweed clung to her skirts. "Should you leave Foxwood, this awaits."

"I don't under—"

She jerked Florence forward, plunging both of them into the pond. Florence gasped, choking on the icy water. She flailed, attempting to free herself.

The woman's grip tightened. She gazed at Florence, unmoved by her struggle.

Florence couldn't even scream. Bubbles of water rushed out of her mouth. She kicked out at her attacker, but her skirts—heavy now with the pond water—curtailed her movements. No matter how she tugged or twisted, the woman's grip on her was relentless, dragging them further, further down.

I'm drowning.

The realisation was as numbing as the water. The murky shadows of the pond blurred, Florence's chest burning with the need for air. Her kicks became weaker.

She would die here, she thought.

But just as suddenly, the grip on her arms released.

Water churned either side of her, hands pulling her to the surface. The brightness of the sky dazzled. Florence gasped.

"Get her to shore." Mr Scott rarely sounded so urgent. "Here."

She was lifted onto the grass and lain on her side. Florence coughed up water and bile.

"Easy." Rosemary's hand was on her shoulder. "You're safe now."

"Frank, I will fetch the doctor. Stay with Rosemary."

"Someone needs to go after Julian." Dawson scanned the fields. "If that woman catches him, who knows what will happen?"

"You mean, if Julian catches her." Rosemary's hands were busy rubbing warmth back into Florence's hands. "Miss

Skelton is our immediate concern. She cannot remain here. She'll catch cold in these damp clothes."

Florence let the words wash over her. Her heart still pounded, her chest heaving with the closeness of her escape. Her throat burned with the agony of her fight for breath. "She… she tried to kill me."

"Why?" Rosemary demanded, leaning over her. Her brown eyes blazed with indignation. "What could anyone have against you?"

Rosemary's dress was as sodden as Florence's, her brown hair plastered against her neck. Was it she who had plunged into the pond to pull her out? The rush of warmth was dizzying. "Rosemary. You saved my life."

8

Dr Goodfellow sat back, putting her stethoscope away. She was a matron of mature years, who paired a man's tweed jacket with her habitual serge walking dress. "Your lungs are clear. Miss Skelton, you have had a very lucky escape."

Florence lay on the living room sofa, heaped with blankets. They had taken away her damp clothes to dry, and she wore her best frock, with her mother's warmest shawl around her shoulders. "All thanks to Miss Scott. If she had not pulled me from the pond, it should be a very different story."

Mr Skelton stood behind the sofa. He placed a hand on Florence's shoulder. "We are much indebted to Miss Scott—and to your prompt help, Doctor."

Florence's mouth fell open. Her father had announced that he would sooner see his family attend a Catholic Church than patronize a female masquerading as a doctor. Had her condition been so serious?

"We are all very lucky," Dr Goodfellow continued. "If the party from Foxwood Court had not passed by when they did, I don't like to contemplate the consequences." She coughed.

"On that note, Lord Cross would like to hear your account of the incident, Miss Skelton. If you do not feel up to it, I can advise him you need rest."

The prospect of being interviewed by stern Lord Cross filled Florence with apprehension. After a moment's thought, she shook her head. "I shall do my best to answer his questions. We must find the woman in the pond before she does herself or someone else an injury."

Her father squeezed her shoulder in approval. "No objections if I remain present?"

"That is for Miss Skelton to decide." Dr Goodfellow eyed her. "Well?"

Florence swallowed. "I should be glad of my father's presence." Better she tell her tale once than have to repeat it.

Lord Cross seemed far too big for the sitting room. He occupied the chair Goodfellow had vacated, sitting on its edge as if eager to pursue the missing woman. "You are certain you are up to this interview, Miss Skelton? I have had a partial account from Mr Scott and his sister."

How bad must she look to have so many people concerned for her? "I am not so shaken that I cannot speak, though there is little that I can tell you." Florence related the events of that afternoon. "I cannot explain it. I had seen the woman only once before and I had not even spoken to her."

"I do not know this woman," Mr Skelton said. "Nor can I think of anyone with a grudge against my daughter. It is more likely that this woman, whoever she is, has some grievance, either against myself or my calling."

"Do you recognise her description?" Lord Cross asked.

"No. Nor did I see her at the lecture." Mr Skelton's fingers tightened on Florence's shoulder. "A vicar's job is not always an easy one. Many times, I have had to break unpleasant truths to parents or spouses of erring souls, and the consequences have not been pleasant. It is possible that this woman knows me from a previous parish and holds some grudge against me, and that she attacked my daughter out of some misguided notion of revenge."

"That is more likely than that your daughter would have an enemy." Lord Cross inclined his head towards her. "The search party sent to find this woman was eager. Every member had nothing but kind words for Miss Skelton."

Florence ducked her head. She should feel flattered, but all she felt was a strange disconnect between her impressions and herself. It was as if she was a puppet, but someone had cut the strings connecting her to reality. "There is no trace of her?"

"None. Julian returned home tired and wet an hour ago. He lost her trail somewhere within the Old Woods." Lord Cross stood. "I shall circulate a description of the woman throughout the county. In the meantime, I wonder whether it might not be a good idea to send your daughters some-where safe. A relative's house, perhaps."

Mr Skelton bowed his head. "I have some such thought in mind." Instead of seeing Lord Cross to the door, he took the chair by the sofa. "Are you tired, Florence?"

From his attitude, he had something of considerable importance to impart. Florence struggled to sit up straighter. "Not so tired that I do not wish to hear what you have to say."

"Yesterday evening, you expressed an interest in earning a living. Mr Temple also spoke of you to me, saying how impressed he was with your modesty and discernment. He wrote to me this morning, offering you the job of secretary companion to himself and his wife." Mr Skelton drew a folded paper from his jacket, turning it over in his hands. "I have mixed feelings. A daughter of mine working smacks of failure, but having seen Dr Good-fellow at work, I must admit there is nothing shameful in a woman doing work that becomes her. Mr Temple is a man of strong Christian values, and your reputation will be

secure in their hands. You would be far from Foxwood—
and this lunatic."

Wait. Was her father really entertaining the prospect of
her employment, or had her near-drowning muddied her
senses? "You propose to let me accept?"

"If it is what you want." Mr Skelton handed over the
letter.

Florence unfolded it with shaking hands.

Dear Horace,

*If I had known that by visiting Foxwood, I would not only
make new friends but reconnect with an old companion, I should
have made the journey years ago. It was a pleasure to relive old
memories with you and meet your charming family. I was especially taken by the sense and modesty of Miss Florence Skelton.*

*Mrs Temple agrees with me that Miss Skelton is the young
woman that we are looking for, possessing not only education
enough to both type and interpret my notes (my handwriting has
not improved since our undergraduate days, so intelligence is
needed to decipher my meaning), but the sensitivity of taste to be a
congenial companion for my wife.*

*Her duties would not be onerous. In the mornings secretarial
work, and in the afternoons keeping Mrs Temple company. I
possess a typewriter and can assure you it is not at all fatiguing for
a lady to use, nor at odds with feminine delicacy. My wife uses it
for the benefit of the charitable societies of which she is a member.*

*In addition to myself and my wife, we have three servants: a
cook, a maid of all work, and a man who acts as a general labourer.
All three have been with my wife since before our marriage and
though taciturn, I have no reason to complain of their behaviour. I
have also engaged the services of a student to assist in my excavations. Mr Vaugham stays in a shepherd's cottage some small
distance from the house. We live a secluded life. The marshes in
which I hope to find proof of the rich heritage of our early ancestors
are deserted. It is half an hour's walk to our nearest village in dry
weather, and a carriage ride from there to the nearest station.*

I offer a salary of 30 pounds a year, payable in quarters, with an advance of two pounds to allow her to outfit herself for the marshes. She will need a good waterproof jacket and at least two pairs of boots as the weather is often wet. If she cares to accept the position, I shall also cover the costs of her travel expenses. I beg that you will let me know your answer at the earliest opportunity.

Your devoted servant,
  Ignatius Temple.

It was real. A job offer—and one her father would allow her to take. Florence stared at the paper. Desolation rushed through her, as wild as the wind rushing over the fields at night. Leave her home, her family, and the kind villagers to earn a living amongst strangers…

Florence dug her fingers into the blanket on her lap. Was it only yesterday she had despaired that her options in life were domesticity or the attic? And here was the chance she longed for, yet she feared to take it. Had Biddy called her brave? How wrong she had been.

Florence sucked in a deep breath.

You must prepare to bury Florence Skelton.

There was a knock at the door. "Is Miss Skelton able to receive visitors?"

Rosemary! Florence gulped, dropping the letter.

Her father opened the door. "As long as you are careful not to overtire her, I can permit it."

Rosemary stepped into the room, her lips pursed. She wore one of Florence's dresses, the drab wool given new life by Rosemary's graceful movements. Her hair fell in loose curls. She held a tea tray. "I have some lemon and honey for your throat."

Saving her life, and now this? "You are too kind."

"I do what anyone would in the circumstances." Rosemary placed the tray on an incidental table and pulled the chair up beside the sofa. She placed the cup in Florence's hands, her warm, rough fingers resting on Florence's.

Rosemary's hands made Florence feel safe. "Thank you."

"What?" Her father's attention was called to the door. "Can't Ashley manage the choirboys himself?" A distant voice protested. The vicar gave way with bad grace. "I must leave you, Florence. You have the bell at your side. If you find yourself tired, you have only to ring it." He gave Rosemary a very brief bow. "Once again, we are indebted to you." He sounded as though the words hurt him.

"He doesn't like me much," Rosemary observed. She let go of Florence's hands, spotting the letter on the floor. "Is this yours?"

Florence looked at it. "A job offer. Mr Temple offers me the role of secretary-companion."

"Splendid!" Rosemary's face glowed. "I have been racking my brains trying to think of a way to free you from your father's thumb, and it falls right into your lap!"

Genuine enthusiasm shone in Rosemary's eyes. Florence felt her heart beat with something that felt very like hope. "You think I should take it?"

Rosemary gripped her hand. "It will be the making of you, Florence Skelton."

Florence was under no illusions. She was not brave… but perhaps she could borrow Rosemary's strength. "If you think so, I shall accept."

9

T he week went by with the bustle reserved for Easter or
Christmas. Florence spent the first few days confined
to her bedroom or the living room. Dr Goodfellow soon
pronounced herself satisfied that Florence had suffered no
lasting harm. So Florence took up her usual duties, with one
difference—either her father, the curate, or the church
warden accompanied her on her errands of mercy.

No one saw the woman in Foxwood, nor sighted her in
any of the surrounding villages. The mystery surrounding
the attack on the vicar's daughter gave way to newer gossip.
When Florence stood on the Rotheram platform, waiting for
her train, only her family waited with her.

Her mother dabbed at Florence's travelling bonnet with a
handkerchief. "Remember, you are a vicar's daughter. Even if
people don't know who you are, you know."

Florence was nervous, but not so nervous she was likely
to forget her identity. "I'll remember."

The vicar glanced at his pocket watch. "Not long now.
Remember to tell the attendant you change trains at
Castleford."

Florence nodded. The prospect of changing trains gave

her apprehension, but admitting her unease felt ungrateful. "I shall be sure to let him know."

Hannah elbowed her. "Now this is a surprise! Look who is here."

With an exuberant shout of greeting, Rosemary dashed up the station steps. "We're in time!" She clasped Florence's hands. "I was so angry at Julian! He takes so long to get ready, I was afraid the train would have come and gone."

"Are you travelling?" Rosemary's dress was too colourful for travelling, nor did she carry a case.

Rosemary's laugh was equal parts scornful and fond. "We're here to see you off, rabbit."

"We?" Florence turned. Mr Scott was explaining to the stationmaster they were not intending to take the train. Mr Dawson brought up the rear with a firm grip on Julian's arm. Had they come to see her?

"It is not every day one sets off to make their own way in the world." Mr Scott removed his hat, giving the vicar a broad grin and Mrs Skelton an effusive bow. "We must mark the occasion. Julian?"

Julian stepped forward, holding out a small, wrapped package. "I hope we'll see you again, Miss Skelton. The other children's helpers aren't half as nice as you are."

Florence hoped her mother and sister hadn't caught that remark. "Is this for me? It's too much."

"A going away present," Mr Scott said. "Julian thought of it himself. A map, so Miss Skelton might know where she is going."

"I always like to know," Julian said.

It was impossible to deny such seriousness. Florence glanced at her father. "How very thoughtful. I accept with thanks."

"Will the train come from that corner? Come, Miss Skelton, let us watch for it together." Rosemary led Florence to the far end of the station platform. "Are you not pleased to see us?" She tucked a strand of hair behind her ear. "You have not smiled."

When Florence's hair escaped, she appeared slovenly. Rosemary looked divine, the curl hinting at her restless nature. "I am astonished. I did not look for so lovely a send-off." Florence blinked, reaching for her handkerchief. "You hardly know me."

"And yet, I feel I know you very well. When I saw you dragged into that pond—" Rosemary's fingers tightened on Florence's arm.

"Don't speak of it," Florence blurted. "I do not like to remember." She had several awful nights, dreams disturbed by the memory of the water clogging her mouth and nose.

"I only wanted to say it was then I realised how dear you were to me." Rosemary drew a small package from her basket and handed it to Florence. "I hope you shall put this to good use."

From its dimensions and solidness, it could only be a book. "I don't know if I can accept this. You know my father's views on literature."

Rosemary snorted. "This is one book your father cannot object to."

Florence felt warmed through and through. Had she had some impact on Rosemary's morals, after all? "Thank you. This means—" she stopped, unable to find the word she wanted.

A shriek split the air, and Florence jumped, almost dropping her parcels. "The train, already?"

A moment more and it was visible, charging down the railway lines towards them. Florence stepped back, but Rosemary remained on the edge of the platform facing it. The gust of the train's arrival swept her skirts and petticoats and tugged at her hair. Rosemary placed her hand on her hat to hold it in place. "I wonder how difficult it is to drive one of these engines?"

The notion was outrageous, lacking all propriety, and so Rosemary that Florence smiled even as her heart sank at the thought of taming so bold a nature. "This is goodbye. If—" She swallowed. "If I should write—"

"I hope you shall. I want to know everything about Aylesport, rabbit, everything." Rosemary reached for Florence's hand, leading her back to her family. "Don't miss the train now."

The stop at Rotheram was brief, Florence the only alighting passenger. The stationmaster and Mr Scott lifted her trunk aboard, and Hannah and Mrs Skelton hugged her.

Her father squeezed her hand and passed her an envelope. "For the journey. Remember, Florence, no matter how distant you are, you carry the honour of our family in your hands."

Florence's 'thank you' stuck in her throat. What was she doing, contemplating such a journey? Work as a secretary? She had not even finished her schooling! Florence's shoulders drooped, and she opened her mouth to protest that she could not go.

But then she noticed Rosemary's eyes resting on her, shining with satisfaction. "You need have no fears there, Mr Skelton. Miss Skelton cannot fail to please."

Rosemary had no doubts. Florence felt her spirits lifted. "I shall not disappoint you, Father." Gripping the metal handrail for support, she climbed on trembling legs into the second-class carriage.

The train did not delay its departure. The whistle blew, the engine starting. With a jolt that almost cost Florence her balance, the train resumed its journey. Florence found her seat, flinging open the window. She just had time to glimpse the group on the platform, lift her hand to wave goodbye, and then they vanished from sight.

And just like that, Florence was alone.

She dropped onto her seat, despair cutting through her

like a knife. Removed from her family and travelling to a distant town where everyone was a stranger. Florence couldn't quite swallow the sob in her throat.

A half hour later, Florence's sorrow abated. She looked out the train window to see a valley sprinkled with daffodils zip past. The people might be unfamiliar, but the scenes she glimpsed from the train window—a dairymaid shooing the herd from the barn, two farmers either side of a fence, snatching a brief conversation—she knew well. Surely Aylesport could not be so different from home.

She dried her eyes and turned her attention to the envelope her father had given her. He'd copied out all the times of her trains, the stations she'd need to change at, and enclosed a half-crown—a whole half-crown—so she might take some refreshment on her journey.

Her mother had wrapped a half loaf, some cake and apples in the basket, along with a bottle of lemonade for her lunch. And there was a dainty embroidered handkerchief, which could only have come from Hannah. Julian had traced Florence's route on the map. She saved Rosemary's gift for last, undoing the string and folding back the brown wrapping paper as slowly as she could.

She disclosed a leather-bound book with no title embossed on its cover. Upon opening it, Florence discovered the pages were blank. A notebook?

The last time she'd had a blank book, it had been an exercise book for school. Florence skated her fingers across the smooth surface of the papers. Her exercise book had seemed to hold so much promise, so much potential. She'd made notes of lectures, written her first compositions, seen the pages fill in her writing… and then her father had consigned the entire notebook to the fire.

She wasn't a schoolgirl now. Florence looked at the pages and her heart sank. What was she supposed to fill it with?

She changed to her second train at Castleford, a porter

carrying her luggage to the next train. Florence's hands shook as she tipped him, but he did not seem to think there was anything amiss in her manner, raising his cap to her with a quick, 'ta, ma'am.' There was a tearoom on the platform and time until her next train. Florence ordered herself a pot of tea.

Cloud came in over the hills as they pulled out of Castleford. The scenery was soon lost in a fog that only grew thicker the further the train progressed. Florence could discern nothing from the train windows. The book of educational tales given to her by her mother as light reading for the train drooped lower on her lap. The prim, self-righteous heroines who never seemed to have a bad thought could not hold her attention. They never did anything! Their claim to goodness rested in self-denial—absenting themselves while those around them fell into peril or succumbed to temptations.

Rosemary would make quick work of those ninnies. Florence glanced around, fearing those around her might discern her sacrilegious thought. The second-class carriage was empty, the last remaining passenger having disembarked at the previous station. Safe!

Rosemary… She'd saved Florence's life, pulling her from the pond with no thought of her own danger. According to Mr Scott, she had hauled Florence to shore before he and Dawson had even reached the edge of the pond. Where were the stories about heroines like Rosemary?

Her gaze fell on the blank notebook. Florence stroked her fingertips over the notebook cover. Dare she?

The vision of Rosemary standing defiant before the vicar with *Jane Eyre* cradled to her bosom came to mind. What more fitting a heroine could there be?

Florence set her pen to paper.

The train pulled out of the station, taking Carmilla away from the few servants remaining faithful to her. She took her seat in the

carriage, pulling the drab shawl she wore closer around her shoul-
ders, disguising her rich auburn locks. The beauty for which she
was famous throughout the district was now no blessing, but a
curse. If she were recognised, all was lost.

I must escape, she thought. Better struggle and ignominy than
marriage to the despicable Baron Crump!

The train whistled a warning as it approached the next
station. Florence didn't hear it. She was far away, taking an
entirely different journey.

10

Words flowed off Florence's pen and onto the page as if she'd turned a tap. She had to force herself to wait for the ink to dry before she could continue her story.

Carmilla came to life, denying grasping suitors, tyrannical guardians, and remaining true to her sense of justice. Nothing daunted her. She found employment as a governess in a house marred by intrigue and—without batting a beautiful eyelid—set about putting Lord Hancock's estate to rights. By the time Florence changed to her final train, Carmilla had befriended the motherless son of her employer, resisted all efforts of Lord Hancock to make her his bride, and had found a bosom companion in his lonely daughter—who, owing to her marked resemblance to his late wife, had to live in the locked up west wing of the Lord's castle. The two women were vowing lifelong friendship when a drop of water hit the page, feathering the ink.

Florence cried out in dismay. Her blotter was in her trunk and she dare not ruin a handkerchief to stop the running ink. She snapped the book shut, looking up to discover the source of the water.

The windows were shut, and the sky, although grey, showed no sign of rain.

A second drop fell on the back of her neck. She glanced up. Something on the luggage rack?

Water gathered at the edges of carriage ceiling, running in streams down the wall. Florence sprang to her feet, discovering a sizeable puddle had spread over the carriage floor without her noticing.

"How—?" Water rose through the corners of the carriage floor, as if the train was mired in a swamp and not rattling down the line at the fast pace it had taken since pulling out of King's Cross.

What's going on? Florence seized the door handle. The handle was rigid, refusing to move. Likewise, the communication cord came away in her hand, loosing a gushing stream into the carriage.

"Let me out!" Florence hammered against the door with her fists. The water was already to her knees, the dampness creeping higher, soaking her skirts and undergarments. The cloth clung to her, threatening to pull her under once again. "Please, help me—someone help me!"

The windows! If she could open the window, she would at least have air. Florence splashed across the carriage. Her lunch basket floated by her, the bottle of lemonade bobbing in the water. Her wet fingers slid across the glass, unable to find purchase.

Nothing for it. She must break it. Florence gathered her strength. She smashed her fist against the glass.

She did not even chip it. The water was now at her breast and rising faster all the time. Florence battered at the window, but the water did not stop coming.

Useless. Florence choked back a sob. Fear caught in her throat. She could already taste the water in her lungs, feel its coldness sapping her strength. This time, there would be no Rosemary to pull her to safety. This time, she would drown.

"Miss?" A rough hand shook her shoulder. "Miss? Can you hear me?"

Florence opened her eyes.

Three strangers looked down at her. The first two wore uniforms identifying them as stationmaster and police officer. The third wore the uniform of the well-bred English gentleman, a tailored suit in a respectable charcoal. The warm tones of his skin indicated he came from a far-off corner of the Empire.

Did she attend a mission event? "I beg your pardon." Florence struggled to sit, but the weight of her soaked skirts hampered her movements. The last thing she remembered was the water rising in the carriage—the carriage!

Florence looked beyond the three men. The second-class carriage was dry, no sign now of the water that had threatened her. The only pool was that disclosed as she sat. "I don't understand. What happened?"

"That's my line." The officer had a gruff voice that made him sound older than his forty-odd years. "When the train stopped at Aylesport and you failed to alight, Mr Vaugham, here to greet you in Mr Temple's place, became concerned." The gentleman inclined his head. "At his request, the stationmaster boarded the train and found you lying unconscious in a puddle."

"And the water?" Florence asked. "What happened to it?"

"Where did it come from, more like." The stationmaster cut in. "Twenty years I've been stationmaster, and a guard I was before that, and never have I seen anything to match it. The window was shut tight!"

"I could not open the window." Memory rushed back. Florence shuddered, pulling her arms around herself. Her cold clothes were no protection against the chill enfolding her. "I was so scared. It made no sense."

"You didn't produce the water, Miss?" The stationmaster's beard was white, but his pursuit of an explanation vigorous. "Then how do you explain why you're clearly wet through?"

"A young lady is not likely to drench herself in cold water at this time of year—or any time of year." Mr Vaugham's tone was scathing. "Miss Skelton has been the victim of some sort of attack."

"Do you know who is responsible for this?" The officer assisted her to her feet. His hands were as cold as Florence's damp garments.

"I saw no one, and I can think of no one who would do such a thing." Florence swallowed a sob. Anyone who could help her was miles away. "I am at a loss to explain this."

A throat cleared. A guard stood in the doorway. "Can I request you remove the lady from the train without further delay? We have a schedule to keep."

The stationmaster bristled. "We've not got to the bottom of this. Where's the guard? How did he not notice anyone entering the carriage? That's what I want to know."

"He told you he saw no one." The guard sounded impatient. "Our passengers are getting restive."

"I do not want to cause any delay," Florence said. "Please. Let us not hold back the train." The sooner she got out of the carriage, the better.

Her lunch basket and its contents were soaked, but her trunk had escaped unharmed. Florence changed into dry clothes in the stationmaster's office and then warmed herself before the waiting room fire. "I cannot offer any explanation. I am as astonished as the three of you."

The police officer looked at his notebook. "Do you wish to file a report?" he asked without enthusiasm.

"Against whom?" Mr Vaugham asked. "She did not see who was responsible."

"Someone did it," the stationmaster insisted. "Our trains are weathertight. Even if the windows were open, no amount of rain could have caused that damage." He slapped his thigh for emphasis. "Sabotage, that's what it is. Damaging railway property."

The police officer snorted. "No doubt the shock of finding herself surrounded by strangers has upset Miss Skelton's memory. More likely she opened the window herself and, when the rain came in, attempted to close it. Her inability to move the window combined with the shock of the communication cord coming loose no doubt overwhelmed her."

"That's not what happened," Florence said. "I remember —" She caught herself. The carriage filling with water was impossible. It had been dry when they'd come to her aid. Only Florence and her belongings had been drenched.

Mr Vaugham glanced out the window. "Given my experience of the English climate, it would not surprise me to learn it capable of spontaneously raining within a railway carriage. That said, the rain has, for the moment, relented. Miss Skelton, I propose we take advantage of this without further delay."

Aylesport village was a short distance from the station. A muddy path connected the two. Florence's trunk was loaded into a wheelbarrow kept at the station for this purpose, and a boy found to wheel it after them. Mr Vaugham strode ahead of Florence, yelling directions back at her. "Keep to the boards. It's always slippery after the rain—and as it always rains around here, the paths are a constant mire."

The boards were little better, thick with algae. Florence had to choose between losing her balance or falling behind her companion. "Mr Vaugham, may I ask you to slow down? I am not as used to navigating these paths as you."

He halted. "My apologies, Miss Skelton. I was thinking not of your comfort, but of the rain."

The clouds were thick above their heads, but Mr Vaugham cast his gaze not at the sky, but at the cottages they passed. Constructed out of stone with roofs thatched with the reeds that grew thick by the side of the river, the houses were thick with moss. Some had what seemed to be flood marks on the building.

Florence saw a few buildings, somewhat larger than the others, which she took to be shops and the stone spire of a church. No one gossiped in the street or browsed the store windows. Did the weather keep the occupants of Aylesport at home?

Florence saw a curtain twitch as they walked by. "Do not worry on my part. I come from a small village, I know well the scrutiny a new arrival receives."

Mr Vaugham glanced at her, surprise visible in his brown eyes. His smile was rueful. "You think me more generous than I am." His shoulders hunched, and he dropped her gaze. "I know well that I am the odd man out in these parts, but I dislike any reminder of it. Foolish I know, but…" His laugh was unconvincing. "Here we are."

They stopped, not at a house, but at a wooden pier. A rowboat was tethered at the end. With the boy's help, Vaugham heaved Florence's trunk into it. She followed, clasping her basket.

"Is it necessary to reach Mr Temple's residence by boat?"

"Only when the rains make the path too dangerous," Vaugham said. "Which is to say most of the time." He untied the dinghy from the dock and sat down to the oars.

Mr Temple had not exaggerated when he said his residence was isolated. The houses of Aylesport were lost to the thick cloud in minutes, replaced by a murky landscape of grass and water. It was hard to tell where one ended and the other began, the river swollen beyond its customary bounds by the rain. Grass poked above the water, waving in the current, while thicker bunches of reeds revealed the river's usual path.

A forlorn cry echoed in the distance, followed by the fluttering of wings. An unseen bird, taking to the air.

Florence shivered, her hand going to her throat. After the experience of the pond, being surrounded by so much water was unnerving. "Is it always like this?"

"When it rains, you cannot see even this much." Mr Vaugham paused, letting the momentum of the boat carry them forward. "I exaggerate. I am told the amount of rain we have experienced this last month is unusual. Though I find there is something to be said for the solitude it enforces." He nodded behind Florence. "Old House."

Florence turned. A stone house of similar make to those of the village, though twice their size, rose out of the mist, its square stone bulk reminiscent of an ancient fort rather than a house. A few side buildings stood at a respectful distance behind it.

Whatever Florence had expected, it wasn't this. She swallowed helplessness, shivering as she felt in the damp air the icy embrace of the pond.

11

A small pier complete with boathouse stood to one side of the house. Mr Vaugham made the boat fast and heaved Florence's trunk onto shore. "I'll return for it with Graham, if you don't mind," he said. "I'm sure you're eager to get inside."

The journey, brief as it had been, was cold. Florence longed for a fire. Yet the stone house had a forbidding air.

Imagination, she told herself. *You're letting the inexplicable events of the afternoon get to you.* She pulled the cloak she had purchased with Mr Temple's advance of her wages closer around herself. She couldn't turn back—her family could not spare the two pounds. "A good idea."

Mr Vaugham ushered her into a dim hall, lighting a candlestick that stood on a press beside the door. "With any luck, we'll find Mr Temple in the study."

A door opened. Mr Temple stepped into the hall, his expression peevish. "There you are, Vaugham. I have been looking for you this past hour. I want—" He stopped still as he took in Florence's presence. "Miss Skelton?"

Florence curtsied. "Good day, Mr Temple." Was he surprised to see her? "I have arrived as your letter directed."

Mr Temple frowned. "I was not expecting you until tomorrow."

"When you did not leave to collect Miss Skelton, we thought you must have mistaken the date," Vaugham said. "I looked for you, but when I did not find you, I went to meet Miss Skelton myself."

A dull red crept across Temple's cheeks. "I have forbidden you from entering the village without my permission."

Florence stepped back. She was used to her father's fury, but Mr Temple's anger was an unknown, more alarming for seemingly coming out of nowhere. "Do not trouble yourself on my part. Mr Vaugham made me feel very welcome."

Mr Temple did not appear to have heard her. "Well, Amit? Have I not made my wishes on the subject clear? There is to be no congress between this house and the village without my permission—none!"

Vaugham stood stiffly. "Yes, sir. But—"

"Do not scold Mr Vaugham, my dear. He left at my direction." A female voice of striking clarity cut through the hall. A woman stood in the shadow at the top of the stairs, her upright carriage giving the impression of height she did not possess. "I did not want Miss Skelton to think herself forgotten."

She descended the stairs with a slow, unhurried carriage, the hall light revealing her to be the beautiful woman of Mr Temple's magic lantern display, dressed now in a full skirted dress of rich carmine stretched over a hoop. At each step, her petticoats rustled, the effect not unlike the trains of royalty in times past. As she neared the bottom of the stairs, she held out her hand.

Mr Temple stepped forward at once to take it. "Miss Skelton, I present my wife, Mrs Temple. Ana, this is Miss Skelton."

Florence had trouble reconciling Mrs Temple's short

stature to her powerful presence. She dropped into a low curtsey, gazing at the floor. She could not have been more awed by the presence of royalty.

"Delighted to meet you." Mrs Temple held out her hand. "I have been looking forward to your company." She turned to her husband. "Miss Skelton will want to freshen up after her journey. I will show her to her room. We will join you for tea in the drawing room."

"As you suggest, my dear." Temple's previous anger had dissipated. "Vaugham, where is Miss Skelton's luggage?"

"Follow me." Mrs Temple led the way back up the stairs.

Florence cast a quick hand over her hair, attempting to pat it back into place. An entirely new source of discomfort replaced her previous apprehension. Mrs Temple was a queen, Florence an inexperienced girl. How on earth could she be a companion to her?

The corridor was dark, swallowing the light of Mrs Temple's candle. "The house is old, a relic of a time when a man's home was his fortress. Being so far remote, we have had little chance to improve it."

"I think it's charming." Florence's voice was breathless, desire to please Mrs Temple warring with her dismay at the length of the corridor. If the passage was so dim now, what would it be like at night with not even the faint light cast by the downstairs windows?

Mrs Temple opened a door. "Your room."

The same grey stone made up the interior walls, softened with rugs on the floor. The thick wooden bed frame was draped in covers, and one narrow aperture admitted the fading afternoon light. A dark-haired woman knelt before the fire in the grate, adding another shovel of peat. Her skin was pale, almost clammy looking.

Florence pressed herself against the wall, biting down on an exclamation of dismay. The woman from the pond!

"Margot will see that your room is clean, and the fire lit," Mrs Temple said. "You do not need help dressing?"

The maid stood, turning her gaze on Florence.

Florence breathed a sigh of relief. She was not the woman from the pond. Now that Florence looked, she could see many differences. Margot was older, a matron rather than a young woman, her features different too. The resemblance was nothing more than the coincidence of pale skin, dark hair, and sombre dress.

Florence realised she was staring. She mustered a smile. "How do you do. No, I don't need help."

Margot inclined her head and left the room.

"She's not talkative," Mrs Temple said. "None of our servants are. I much prefer silence to meaningless chatter."

Florence nodded, cheeks flaming. "I quite agree."

"Margot will light your fire and bring the tea tray at eight. Ignatius starts his work at ten. You will be ready to start with him. We take luncheon at two, and then you will join me in the drawing room. We dine at seven, after which your time is your own. Does that suit, Miss Skelton?"

Florence's head whirled. "Admirably."

There was a creak on the floor outside. "That must be Mr Vaugham and Graham with your luggage."

Florence opened the door. Mr Vaugham and an older man entered, bearing her trunk between them. Mr Vaugham was a slight man, but he was taller than Graham—a wizened old man whose black hair was peppered through with white. His knuckles were an angry red and his palms rough with decades of work, but his skin had the same clammy absence of colour as the maid.

A regional thing, Florence decided, making way for the trunk. Or was the weather as bad as Mr Vaugham claimed? "Thank you, Mr Vaugham. Mr Graham, how do you do."

Mr Vaugham nodded, but Graham did not appear to hear

her words. He gave a nod to his mistress and tramped out of the room.

"We'll leave you to get settled in," Mrs Temple said. "I will be back to guide you to the drawing room."

Mr Vaugham held open the door for her. He waited for Mrs Temple to move out of earshot and then turned back. "May I take the liberty of a quick word in private, Miss Skelton?"

Florence's heart sank. Another proposal? "Yes, Mr Vaugham?"

"I have not spoken of the strange accident you encountered on the train," Mr Vaugham said in low tones. "Mr Temple is put on edge by unexpected events. The slightest change to his schedule can upset him all day. I leave the decision on whether to mention it to you, but it is my advice that you do not."

That was much more thoughtful than Florence had expected. "Thank you. I shall let your experience guide me."

He gave her a slight smile and bowed. "I'll see you downstairs." He shut the door behind him.

Florence let out a breath and looked around her.

In Mrs Temple's absence, the room felt much bigger. There was a washbasin in one corner, and a press which would be more than adequate for her belongings. Florence surveyed herself in the glass. In changing out of her damp garments, she'd not had time to press her day dress, and it had become even further rumpled in the boat. No wonder Mrs Temple suggested she freshen up.

She opened her trunk, removing her damp dress and garments and spreading them out before the fire. If Mr Temple had not liked so small a change as Mr Vaugham collecting her from the station, she did not like to think of his reaction to the astonishing manner of her arrival. She contrived to find a dress that was not too damp and shook out the wrinkles. She hung up her remaining wardrobe and turned her attention to her basket.

"Oh, no!" The notebook Rosemary gave her was wet through and through, the pages sticking together. Florence beheld the running ink and felt tears surge anew.

Ruined! She might be out of her father's reach, but once again her writing had come to an abrupt end.

Mrs Temple did not exaggerate. Margot brought Florence's tea in the morning stony-faced, ignored thanks and greeting both, and lit the fire in complete silence. She left the room as silently as she'd arrived.

Florence was not used to lying abed in the morning. She washed and dressed, drinking her cup of tea before the fire. At least Margot's silence had this to recommend it: Florence had not had to explain the clothing drying before the fire.

Perhaps no explanation was necessary. Rain fell, a steady trickle that dimmed the ears even as cloud obscured the sky and mist hung thick over the bog. Old House was as remote as if it occupied not a marsh but an island.

Florence made her way downstairs at nine o'clock to find breakfast served. Mr Temple looked up from his letters to enquire if she'd slept well, and, upon finding that she had, read her several headlines that had caught his attention.

Mr Vaugham arrived soon after, raindrops resting on his hair, giving him the aspect of an alert otter. "I scarcely need my coffee this morning. In this weather, the walk from my cottage is wash and exercise combined."

Florence had forgotten Mr Vaugham occupied a cottage rather than the house. "Is your cottage far from here?"

"Not too far," Mr Temple said. "Mr Vaugham is no admirer of our English weather, Miss Skelton. He likes to complain."

Mr Vaugham's eyes glittered. "Mine will not be the only complaints come evening unless this rain lifts. Just wait. Mr Temple, for all his pride in his home country, does not enjoy damp any more than the next man."

Florence glanced at the windowpane. Rivulets flowed unrelenting across the glass's surface. "You do not intend to work in that? You will catch cold."

"We are well protected. We wear two layers of wool and oilskins," Mr Temple assured her.

No wonder he had insisted that Florence bring wet weather clothing! Florence's heart sank as she assessed her wardrobe against the downpour.

"Do not look so dismayed, Miss Skelton. Your task is here, in the library." Mr Temple consulted his watch. "There is just time for me to instruct you in the typewriter's use."

Florence had not yet finished her breakfast, but she set aside her toast. The typewriter filled her with trepidation.

The machine was about the size of a bread bin with keys that made an alarming clacking sound when pressed. Florence found them loud, and the ringing of the return handle clamorous.

Mr Temple showed her how to set the paper and change the ink ribbon. "To start, I suggest familiarising yourself with the machine by practicing. The quick brown fox jumped over the lazy dog."

Florence looked at the array of keys before her. "And once I have done that?"

"You'll type up my field notes first." Temple inspected one of the study bookcases, flicking through leather-bound volumes until he found what he sought. He placed a much-battered notebook beside Florence. "Here. Do you have any questions, Miss Skelton?"

"If I run into any difficulties with the machine, is there any who can assist me?"

"Mrs Temple is proficient with it," Mr Temple assured her. "She rises about ten, though I am sure that so apt a pupil as yourself will have no issue."

Florence nodded, feeling herself an imposter. What knew she of machines?

Alone with the typewriter, she placed a single finger on the key. *thequickbrownfox…* No, that wasn't right.

It took a bit of practice, but Florence figured out how to insert spaces, and, at length, how to make capital letters. Feeling much more hopeful, she propped the first field journal open before her and began to type.

It was slow going. Florence wasn't learning just the machine, but Mr Temple's handwriting and his methods. More than once she stopped to puzzle over a word. Frequent stains showed Mr Temple's notebook had fared no better against the Aylesport weather than hers had in the train.

She learned that Mr Temple believed the goods he had uncovered so far were only the tip of the iceberg. The varied nature of his finds—including weapons, pottery shards, and jewellery—indicated they were funerary offerings for an important figure to the bog's primitive inhabitants. He'd identified three probable locations for the grave of the deceased, and had tackled the largest first, a long-raised barrow that rose out of the bog about a twenty-minute walk from Old House. Mr Temple had found more pottery shards and uncovered groundworks and planks, suggesting a building once occupied the site. He predicted a great discovery was just around the corner.

Florence glanced at the date. Five years ago.

A long time to be searching.

Mr Temple and Mr Vaugham returned for lunch, chilled

to the bone, with steam rising from their clothes as they stood by the fire.

"No finds," Mr Temple said in response to Florence's question. "But every excavation brings us closer to our object. I do not doubt that she is out there somewhere."

"She?" Florence followed his gaze out the window to the bog. "The queen from your lecture?"

Mr Temple beamed. "I am flattered you remember. Yes, though I cannot be certain she was a queen. All we know is that she was someone of great importance to the inhabitants of this swamp, and, should we find her, of unparalleled importance to British archaeology—to our very under-standing of our nation."

"Providing that she is real," Mr Vaugham cut in. "It is my theory, Miss Skelton, that we have not found the resting place of a mortal but the temple of a goddess. The ancient Celts worshipped nature in feminine form, and the objects we have uncovered may be religious offerings."

"Not this again!" Mr Temple protested. "The ordinary nature of some of the goods, and indeed, the signs of wear on the weapons, proves these were used in life by she who they accompany in death. An object made purely as an offering—"

"We cannot assume the ancients gave only purpose-made objects as offerings," Mr Vaugham countered. "Who is to say that a warrior, upon returning from battle, might not offer the sword that protected him to the bog?"

"Protected *her*," Mr Temple corrected. "The majority of weapons were made for a woman—and the same woman, going by their size."

Mr Vaugham's brow furrowed, clearly unconvinced.

Florence had not forgotten Mr Temple's outburst the night before. She cut in before Mr Vaugham could prolong the argument. "I do not understand. Should not a sword rust away to nothing in the bog?"

"Anywhere else, yes. But these waters have a special property." Mr Temple turned to Florence with a beneficent air. "The layers of peat are so thick, no light penetrates beyond the surface of the bog. When new peat forms, old peats dissolves, forming an acidic substance that, combined with the lack of oxygen in the bog, creates an environment with unique preserving properties—much like peat itself makes such a useful source of fuel."

Florence tried to look as though she understood. "And you think the bog will preserve a body as it has weapons and pottery?"

He nodded. "Bodies have been found in bogs in Ireland and Denmark so fresh they were mistaken for recent murder victims. The discovery of the Danish body revitalised the study of the Iron Age in that country. A similar discovery here would transform archaeology."

A gong sounded. "Luncheon," Mr Temple announced. "This way, Miss Skelton."

The dining room was better lit than the other rooms in Old House, thanks to the fact that its high ceiling hosted a predecessor to the chandelier, a circular candle holder held aloft by the wooden ceiling beams.

After lunch, Mrs Temple indicated that she intended to walk. "Will you join me, Miss Skelton? I imagine you'd like to learn your surroundings."

The cloud was not inspiring, but the rain had slowed to scattered showers rather than the steady downpour of the morning. Florence agreed that a walk would be pleasant and changed into her warmest dress and waterproof cloak.

Mrs Temple led the way past the small pier and boathouse and along a muddy track across the grass. A few cows grazed the field behind Old House, the ropes around their necks attached to metal pins driven into the earth.

"It is easy to lose your way in the marsh," Mrs Temple said. "We must take precautions to ensure our cattle do not fall victim to the waters." She led the way, not seeming to need any help navigating the marsh herself.

Florence followed closely behind, watching where Mrs Temple placed her feet. "How do you know the way?" Once they'd left the dairy and stables behind, the path gave way to grass and clusters of moss and weed.

Mrs Temple pointed. "Do you see that wooden marker?"

Florence spotted a stick poking out of a cluster of moss. "Where does this path lead?"

"It joins us to our nearest neighbour, and from there to the village," Mrs Temple explained. "You may wander this far by yourself, but no farther."

No farther? Florence looked to the next marker with a sense of dismay. Even after the attack on her at the pond, her parents had not forbidden Florence from walking where she liked. Being able to take exercise was one of her few pleasures. "Only this far? I assure you, I would be very careful."

"No matter how much care you took, the risk would be too great." Mrs Temple turned back to the house. "Let us return."

As she traipsed after Mrs Temple, a gust caught Florence's bonnet, tugging it from her head. "My hat!" She sprang after it.

"Do not take another step!" Mrs Temple shouted.

Florence paused in shock—and realised Mrs Temple's meaning. Her right foot was sinking fast into mud disguised by a top layer of thick moss. Her left foot was yet on solid ground. Florence attempted to pull her foot free, but discovered the mud weighed it down.

"Give me your hand." Mrs Temple took Florence's hands and pulled her back onto the path. "You see? The marsh is treacherous."

"I'm sorry." Florence's cheeks flushed red with embarrassment, even as she eyed her skirts and stockings with dismay. The mud was black and smelled of rot.

"Wait here. Do not move from the path." Mrs Temple strode back to the boatshed, returning with a long wooden pole with a hook on the end. "Should you ever lose something in the marsh, use this to retrieve it." She used the hooked pole to fish Florence's bonnet from the vile-smelling mud. She shook the mud from the bonnet before handing it back to Florence. "I suggest we end our walk here. We do not want the swamp to claim another victim."

Florence looked up from her battered bonnet with alarm. "Another victim—someone has died here?"

"Oh, many someones," Mrs Temple said. "That is to say, if my husband's theories are correct. Bogs are dangerous places, Miss Skelton, even to those who know them well. The village people will not go out in them alone. You would be wise to follow their example." Mrs Temple turned, leading the way back to the house.

Cradling her bonnet, Florence followed. She no longer felt like walking.

13

Mrs Temple bade Florence read aloud to her from the newspaper as she occupied herself with her needlework. Rather than a companion, she wanted entertainment while she worked.

This suited Florence. Mrs Temple was so removed from her in age, beauty and composure that being her companion was a nerve-wracking prospect. Reading aloud was something she could do. Even so, she was relieved when dismissed to freshen up for dinner.

A companion did not dress for dinner, but Florence brushed her hair and made sure she was as neat as she could be. This did not take long. She checked that her clothes had dried and folded them away.

She'd left her notebook in front of the fire, pages fanned out. A few stuck together, but mostly they were dry. Florence flicked through the pages. Many of her sentences were lost to the water, but enough remained that she thought she might be able to recreate it.

Carmilla's not done yet—and neither am I. Florence placed the book with her belongings and made her way to dinner, her spirits rising.

Mr Temple made it a rule not to talk about his work at the dinner table, but he and Mr Vaugham found plenty of other things to argue about, from politics to literature, even to the next day's weather. Florence listened in mute horror, sure that Mr Temple would dismiss his assistant at any moment. She looked across the table. Surely, Mrs Temple must share her horror? Her hostess seemed lost in thought. She stirred only when Margot asked her if they were ready for the next course.

Was this usual? Florence's heart sank. She did not know if she could endure it.

She must. There was the two pounds to earn back, to say nothing of her family's approbation. Having fought to have a job of her own, she could not return to Foxwood prematurely.

After dinner, Mr Vaugham returned to his cottage and Mr and Mrs Temple settled with his reading and her sewing in the drawing room. Florence gathered up her courage. "Will you permit me to make use of the typewriter? I should like to practice it."

Mr Temple looked up from his book. "You will not be too tired, Miss Skelton? I do not wish to overwork you."

Florence shook her head. "I should like to try it. I have a notebook that was—" She remembered the Temples did not know of her accident. "Water-damaged. I want to type up my thoughts while they are still fresh. I can pay for the paper I use."

"Nonsense," Mr Temple said. "Your practice is of benefit to me. If that is how you would like to spend your evening, I shall have a fire lit in the study for you."

The silent Margot lit the fire and Florence sat down to the typewriter, feeling a flush of nervous excitement. Her fingers shook as she lifted them to the machine.

Take hold of yourself! It was not like this morning when the machine had been new. Florence typed.

Carmilla's adventures took shape much faster than Mr Temple's notes had. Florence did not need to decipher the text, Carmilla coming back to her in all her flame-haired glory. In fact, even when Florence could read the words of her notebook, she didn't type exactly what was written. She expanded it, adding weight and description. By the time her candle was in danger of burning out, Florence had typed almost half of the notebook pages, and her head was full of Carmilla's next steps. She must extricate Miss Hancock from her prison, that was certain, but before she could do that, she needed a safe house to hide her. The problem of how to do this still occupied Florence as she climbed into bed.

Morning—and the return to work—came as a complete surprise.

Florence grew accustomed to her new life. Typing up Mr Temple's field notes grew easier as she became more familiar with both his work and the typewriter. She still came across paragraphs or words that required help to render in type, but those became increasingly more occasional. Mrs Temple did not demand more from Florence than her voice, and she had ample time to devote to the unfolding story of Carmilla. Her heroine took on as real a presence as anyone at Old House, giving Florence a taste of the friendship she lacked.

Or did Carmilla bring to mind her model? Florence paused one night to look at the page she'd just finished typing. Rosemary was never far from her thoughts. She both longed for and feared Rosemary's reaction to her story. Would she consider it foolish, or was this how she'd hoped Florence would use her gift?

Florence lay her hand flat against the pile of typed papers. There was only one way to find out.

Tomorrow was a red-letter day for two reasons. Not only was it Florence's day off, but it was her first payday. She knew exactly what to do with her salary. She would send the bulk to her parents, but Mr Temple had arranged for a bank account in her name where she might start some savings of her own. Then there was the post office, where she would purchase a manuscript box to take her pages.

After breakfast, Florence tucked her manuscript into her basket and made her way downstairs. There had been several days without rain, and she hoped the water would have receded enough for her to make the journey to the village.

Mr Temple emerged from his study as she passed. "Is that you, Ana? Oh, I beg your pardon, Miss Skelton." He frowned as he took in her basket. "You do not think of going anywhere?"

Something in his tone that made Florence uneasy. She forced a smile. "I was hoping to go to the village. It is my day off, and I have some errands—"

"Out of the question," Mr Temple said. "It is too dangerous."

"I would stick to the path—"

"We do not yet know there is a path to stick to. The wooden markers have a way of being dislodged by the rain. It is necessary to periodically replace them. I should not risk one as new to the marshes as you are to the path at present, Miss Skelton." Mr Temple motioned to her basket. "You have letters to post? Leave them to Graham. He will make the journey on your behalf."

"I would very much like to go with Graham," Florence started.

He shook his head. "I promised your parents I would take good care of you. They would not approve of you roaming unsupervised in the village."

Florence's throat felt tight, the bottom of her mouth sour. "At home I often walked through the village on errands."

Mr Temple smiled, but there was steel in his voice. "Ah, but in Foxwood you were known as the vicar's daughter, and thus inviolate. Here you are unknown, and you do not have your father's reputation to protect you."

"How am I to become known if I do not—"

"You will not go to the village," Mr Temple snapped. "Not today, not unless I grant you permission. Do you understand?"

Florence flinched. "I—yes, Mr Temple. I do."

He smiled, his good humour restored. "I am glad. Go upstairs and remove your bonnet. You will not need it today. I'll send Graham to collect your letters."

"The stamp—"

"I'll arrange it with Graham."

"I lack an envelope of suitable size—"

"No matter how many pages your letter, there will be something in the study to suit. Do not distress yourself another moment, Miss Skelton."

Florence swallowed. She could not show Mr Temple her pile of pages without exciting curiosity. Nor could she admit to writing fiction. "You are right, Mr Temple. I'll see what I can find."

She entered the study, opening the desk drawers with little hope.

A throat cleared behind her. "May I offer some unsolicited advice?"

Florence whirled around. "I did not see you there, Mr Vaugham."

"I wished to be unnoticed." Mr Vaugham had drawn the curtains, secreting himself in the window seat. "Mr Temple is apt to forget that I have the day off and think of errands for me. I find it good practice to be as invisible as possible."

Florence knew little about young men besides that they were a source of temptation and a constant trial to Christian women. She'd not expected they would hide themselves away like a child—or like Jane Eyre. She tilted her head. "Is that your advice?"

"No." Mr Vaugham glanced at the closed door and lowered his voice. "Mr Temple is in a foul mood. An article in the latest volume of the Historian's Companion referenced the Aylesport Lady and heaped scorn on his method."

"The Aylesport Lady?" Florence repeated.

"The bog body. Found here a few years ago." Mr Vaugham frowned. "I thought everyone knew of it."

There was no window in the room and the door was closed but a chill travelled down Florence's spine. Or was that the memory of clammy hands at her neck? "Is she still here?"

Mr Vaugham blinked. "No. She's in the museum at Hartlea. Mr Temple won't have her talked about in his presence. The whole incident was a serious blow to his reputation."

"Tell me, please." Florence stopped, shocked at her own daring.

Mr Vaugham glanced again at the door. "You're sure?"

Florence hesitated. She did not want to anger Mr Temple further by learning something he had forbidden even being discussed. Then again, was it not better she knew what to avoid? Florence's shoulders slumped. That is the choice of Eve! Knowledge or blissful ignorance.

Cold words brush her ear. *I am your future. Should you leave Foxwood, this is what awaits.* Florence swallowed. This was no mere moral dilemma. "I must know."

14

"I have an envelope I think might hold your papers in my cottage," Mr Vaugham suggested. "The walk should give us a chance to talk."

Going anywhere unaccompanied with a bachelor was courting ruin, but to accompany him to his residence was damning herself. Florence knew there was only one reply to make to his invitation.

And yet, Mr Vaugham had been kind to her, and this might be her only chance to learn of the Aylesport lady—whoever she was. "That sounds pleasant."

Florence was already wearing her bonnet and gloves so they set off without delay. Vaugham's cottage was visible from Old House, a dirt path leading the way to it.

Mr Vaugham strode ahead. It seemed to be his usual manner. He collected himself, returning to her side. "Forgive me. I'm not used to company."

Florence felt better. Someone intending to ruin her would surely be more attentive. "The Aylesport lady?"

"Yes." Mr Vaugham dug his hands into the pockets of his coat. "I saw an allusion to it in a letter responding to one of

Mr Temple's articles. I asked him about it, and he swore at me. It was the first time I'd seen him in a rage."

Florence could well imagine his shock. "Did he explain?"

"No. Told me to mind my business. But I had to know more. My next day off, I made the trip to Hartlea to see the museum. The curator gave me the complete story. A few years ago, the body of a young woman was found in the bog. Mr Temple was on hand when it happened and claimed she was a Celtic woman from the tribe who inhabited these lands. He was all set to publish a paper on her when a visiting archaeologist who had heard of the find wanted to see the Celtic princess. He noted that the body showed no signs of the discolouring written about in accounts of foreign bog bodies and pushed for a closer examination. It was then Mr Temple discovered his ancient young woman had a modern false tooth."

Florence frowned. "She wasn't ancient?"

Mr Vaugham nodded. "No one knows who she was or where she came from, but she can't have been more than twenty years old. Whatever clothing she had was lost to the swamp, so that was no help in identifying her."

"What about the preserving properties Mr Temple spoke of?"

"They cannot be relied upon," Mr Vaugham said. "When the conditions align, they are remarkable. The woman, for what it's worth, looked as though she'd died yesterday."

Florence caught her breath. "You saw her?"

"Indeed. The remains are on display."

Florence stumbled. "That can't be decent!"

"It's historic," Mr Vaugham turned to look at her. "And she's covered. Not that a dead woman has much concern for modesty."

"She is still a woman," Florence said. "It isn't—it isn't proper." Her eyes burned. She blinked. "Dead or not, to be displayed like one was a thing… It's heartless!"

"History isn't about feelings but about facts. This woman may have family or friends searching for her. If someone identifies her, she can be laid to rest."

"Surely she can be identified without being displayed in such a way." Florence bunched her hands into fists. "This just seems wrong."

Vaugham seemed startled. "You feel strongly about this, Miss Skelton."

Florence pulled herself together. A well brought up lady never expressed powerful emotion. "I beg your pardon." They had reached the cottage. "I'll take in the air out here."

"Don't leave the path," Vaugham cautioned. "I won't be a moment."

Florence looked back at Old House. The day was fine for once, the ever-present cloud replaced by steam rising from the wet grass. The clumps of moss and reeds looked inviting with no water in sight, but Florence had no wish to wander.

Mr Vaugham closed the cottage door. "The envelope." He held out a good-sized envelope of sturdy card.

"Thank you. That suits my purposes." Florence hesitated to take the envelope. "I must apologise. The liberty I took talking to you earlier—"

"The apology is mine." Vaugham inclined his head. "History has been for me a refuge from harsh realities. I view it as a realm unconnected with my world. The reminder that we cannot separate history from the people who lived it is one I needed."

Her lack of self-control had not disgusted him? Or perhaps he was simply willing to overlook it. Florence took the envelope. "It is generous of you to pretend you have anything to learn from myself."

"There is no pretence," Vaugham said. "I make a point never to elaborate on or alter facts. To be a historian is to record the truth as accurately as possible, ensuring that one's conclusions are unassailable."

Florence walked in silence for a moment, digesting this. "You fear your work will be attacked?"

"It must be. When an unknown historian—or any historian—publishes his findings, the academic community reviews it. Any mistake or error is interrogated, more so when the writer has some startling discovery to disclose."

Florence looked across the mossy field to Old House. "Is that what happened to Mr Temple?"

"Indeed. He did not publish his paper, but the damage was done. The other archaeologist talked, and word got round. A satirical article was published making fun of Mr Temple's error, and he retired from public lectures for a few years." Mr Vaugham eyed the approaching cloud. "The curator told me that Mr Temple tried to have the body removed from display, and, when the museum refused, insisted his name not be associated with it. He is a proud man, and he does not take any reminder of his failure well."

Florence nodded, strolling down the path. How many times had her father lectured against the sin of pride? "If to be a historian is to be held up to such high standards, I do not know why anyone should choose such a profession."

"It is because of those high standards that it calls to me." Mr Vaugham strode ahead with his customary energy. "In my articles, my papers, my letters, I am judged by my work. No one knows anything more of me than my name and my argument. I must prove myself, and I do. Whereas if I leave this house and go into the village, I am judged before I can even say a word in my defence."

Florence tucked a lock of hair behind an ear. "Is it so bad as that? Surely once the people know you—"

Mr Vaugham shook his head. "It doesn't matter what I say or do. They view me according to their notions of what an Indian is. Should I live in this village my entire life, I might be tolerated, but accepted—never."

"I am sorry to hear that." Florence hesitated. Her acquaintance with Mr Vaugham was slight, and yet… "I do not think you mean to spend the rest of your life in Aylesport."

He laughed. "God, spare me! No, I have greater ambitions. I intend to build a reputation for myself working somewhere so isolated my academic peers will have no notion of the fact that Mr A. Vaugham is not an Englishman. By the time they learn, my work will be unshakeable, and they can have no cause to remove me from their ranks."

"Is that why you argue with Mr Temple so much?"

Vaugham bowed his head. "You have found me out. Many of the arguments I use on him are those I fear would be applied to my work. I must have a robust defence—and the best defence I have found is the truth."

Florence adjusted her bonnet, a frown on her face. She disliked Mr Temple and Mr Vaugham's arguments, but this put them in a new light. "Mr Temple doesn't mind?"

"No. He knows that he must face the scrutiny of his peers and the public. He invites questions at his lectures, so he must prepare to answer them."

As they passed the dairy, a shape stepped out of the shadows and joined them. "Who must I prepare to answer?"

"Mr Temple!" Florence's mind retraced their conversation. Had anything been said that could cast a critical light on their employer?

Mr Vaugham took the sudden appearance in stride, nodding to Mr Temple. "I've just been telling Miss Skelton that a historian is sometimes called upon to defend his work."

Florence willed her heart to stop racing and nodded. "I am no longer surprised you go about your archaeological explorations with such care or record them in such detail. Mr Vaugham has explained to me how important it is that your findings be as accurate as possible."

Mr Temple seemed pleased. "Not just accurate, but correct." He fell into step besides Florence. "Facts alone can mislead. We must interpret them according to a worthy principle. A historian should not just educate but elevate. My findings will inspire new pride in the English, encouraging them to see themselves anew in light of the accomplishments of their distant ancestors."

Vaugham snorted. "You must prove those accomplishments first."

"I will—I have no doubt of that." They'd reached the steps of Old House. Graham stood by the door, wearing his usual scowl. Temple turned to Florence. "Do you have your letters ready to go?"

"One moment. Mr Vaugham was kind enough to give me an envelope, but I must address it." Florence ran inside to the study. She feared to consign her story to the mail in front of Mr Temple but failing to produce a letter would excite more curiosity than the sight of a bulky envelope. Her hands shook as she wrote Rosemary's name and address. What she did was wrong. She could not even pray for God's deliverance.

For once, luck was on her side. When she returned to the steps, Mr Vaugham and Mr Temple were engaged in a discussion so heated neither saw Florence pass her package to Graham. The manservant trudged towards the boat without another word.

Florence watched him bear her story out into the world. It was too late now to take it back, even though she longed to. And yet, another part of her was glad it was out of her hands. There was nothing to do now but wait for Rosemary's reply.

15

Waiting for the mail was a new form of torture. At Foxwood, Florence at least had distractions in the form of her family and parish concerns. Her employment at Aylesport claimed her time, not her mind, leaving her thoughts to run rampant.

Would Rosemary approve of the story? Would she recognise herself in Carmilla? Had Florence taken an unforgivable liberty in drawing her heroine?

What if in her writing she'd revealed just how little she knew of the world? Or worse—laid her own cowardice bare? Rosemary must be disgusted… Florence heaved a sigh.

Mrs Temple looked up from her sewing. "I did not think Mr Pickwick's adventures so tiring, Miss Skelton. Would you prefer to read something different?"

Florence blushed, picking up the book on her lap. "I beg your pardon. I did not sleep well last night." She read again, forcing her mind to focus on the words. This worked well enough during the day, but once she extinguished her candle and pulled her covers up to her chin, there was no respite from her wonderings. What must Rosemary think of her?

Deliverance came at last. One evening, Graham entered the drawing room with a pile of letters.

"A veritable cornucopia of correspondence," Mr Temple crowed. He was in good spirits, having trounced Mr Vaugham's assertion that Cambridge would win the boat race this year. "A periodical for me, a letter from your father, Mr Vaugham, the usual update from the society of right-thinking woman—and two letters for Miss Skelton."

Florence held out a hand for her letters, but Mr Vaugham, smarting from his defeat, looked up truculently.

"You cannot assume that a letter for me is from my father."

"I do not assume." Mr Temple's eyes sparkled. "As a historian, I gather the facts and make my observations." He held up an envelope with an Indian postmark. "The handwriting is decisive, written in the expansive hand of a thinker—as I know your father to be. Moreover, the return address is the Calcutta mission—"

"The return address gives the thing away entirely." Mr Vaugham pushed his plate away in disgust.

Mr Temple shook his head. "Handwriting and choice of writing implement, even the quality of paper and the ink an individual uses, all says much about the writer, much more than he or she reveals."

Florence's heart sank. What did her writing reveal about her? "What do you mean, Mr Temple?"

"To a point, yes." Mr Vaugham rallied. "But in this household, with our stationery supplied by you, sir, paper and ink cannot reveal anything about myself or Miss Skelton, or even Mrs Temple."

Mrs Temple looked up from her sewing. "Would not the similarity reveal a common origin, allowing someone to infer the makeup of our household?"

"I propose we test this," Mr Temple said. "As Mr Vaugham and Miss Skelton are both well acquainted with my handwriting, Ana, we will make you the judge of this experiment. Mr Vaugham and Miss Skelton, come with me to the study."

Mr Temple found writing implements and paper for all three of them. "We shall see if Ana can identify the writer by their handwriting alone."

"Not just their handwriting," Mr Vaugham protested. "Word choice, vocabulary, all of that must play a part in identification."

Mr Temple rubbed his hands together. He looked like a child at a birthday party, pleased as punch with his experiment. "In that case, I shall dictate a generic message all three of us shall write."

Florence caught herself tapping the floor with one foot. She stilled the gesture. Eager as she was to receive her mail, she did not want to communicate her impatience to Mr Temple. She picked up her pen.

Mr Temple stroked his chin. "Due to an unforeseen and urgent matter, I must take my leave. I apologise for my abrupt departure and pray I do not cause too untoward an inconvenience. I will send instructions for the removal of my belongings once I have a fixed address." He eyed Mr Vaugham. "Is there anything you object to?"

Mr Vaugham shook his head, concentrating, like Florence, on capturing the words. "Can you read that again?"

Once all three papers were completed, they were set before Mrs Temple. She picked up Mr Temple's. "It has been many years since I acted as your secretary, but I could not fail to recognise your writing, my dear Ignatius."

"I thought as much," Mr Temple said. "Still, Mr Vaugham and Miss Skelton's writing must be new to you."

"Indeed." Mrs Temple looked at the two pages. She tapped one. "Mr Vaugham." She tapped the other. "Miss Skelton."

"That is correct," Florence said. "How did you know?"

Mrs Temple looked down at the pages. "This handwriting appears more fluid, more confident—it is the hand of someone who writes often enough to be careless. Look how the words flow into each other."

Mr Vaugham's mouth twisted. "Guilty as charged."

"Miss Skelton writes with great care to form each letter neatly and evenly. I would say she is a thorough and attentive scholar."

Florence shook her head. "Untried would be more accurate. I would think Mr Vaugham takes great pains with his work."

"Agreed." Mr Temple picked up the two pages. "Your writing is no accurate reflection of your work. I concede the argument—in your case, at least, handwriting is no reflection of ability."

"This small sample cannot produce accurate results. We should need a greater number of samples and a judge who does not know us so well as Mrs Temple," Mr Vaugham started.

Florence picked up her two letters from the tray. "If no one objects, I shall read my letters in my room."

The gentlemen did not even appear to hear her, but Mrs Temple gave a slight nod. Florence wasted no time. She sank onto her bed, hands shaking as she turned the letters over. She recognised Hannah's handwriting on the first, but the second was unfamiliar. The envelope was stiff, quality card, embossed with the Cross family shield.

Rosemary! Florence's fingers trembled as she broke the seal.

Dearest Rabbit,

Didn't I say your job would be the making of you? I adore Carmilla and was never more pleased than with her refusal of Lord Hancock. Such spirit! Such truth, uttered with such boldness! I do not think you should have dared pen such a speech under your father's roof. Do I infer that your employment with the Temples goes well? I am glad. I think about you often and wonder how you fare. Your letter was very welcome.

Florence exhaled, shutting her eyes and falling backwards onto her bed. She clutched the letter to herself. Rosemary—pleased! And not just pleased, approving! Her joy was complete.

And there was more of the letter to read. Florence held up the papers.

I could not resist making my own additions to your manuscript. I hope you will forgive my poor scribblings. Mr Dawson says that with diligent practice, I shall improve. I hope so! I do not think I could get any worse.

Scribbles? Florence turned over the papers she held. A collection of sketches greeted her—Rosemary had illustrated scenes from Florence's manuscript. There was Carmilla, head held aloft, while Lord Hancock begged on one knee for her hand. Rosemary had captured both Carmilla's spirit and Hancock's grasping character. Then there was the moment Carmilla discovered the forgotten Miss Hancock in her prison. Florence blinked back tears at the glow of happiness evident in Miss Hancock's face. To have a friend after so many years alone…

Rosemary had not simply liked her work, she had understood it. Her illustrations showed that she shared Florence's zest for Carmilla.

Hardly daring to allow herself to feel such happiness, Florence turned back to the letter.

My art lessons are the only thing that makes Foxwood bearable, barring Julian, and even then, I resent how much of my brother's time his lessons take. I know I am unfair. My brother must have employment, and Julian is so agreeable a pupil, and Lord Cross and Mr Leighton such thoughtful employers. But it is difficult to go from being all-in-all to each other to having so small a portion of my brother's time. I would resent Mr Dawson—sometimes I do, for the claims his friendship has on Basil—but he is unfailingly kind to me and does not let on he notices my rudeness. This makes me angrier. What a relief to dive into Carmilla's world and live her adventures with her. Until I can find proper employment of my own, books and walks are my only escape.

Florence reread the paragraph. Her heart ached. She could well imagine Rosemary's expansive spirit chafing under such constraints. Even so, to speak so openly of her private troubles was not quite proper... Was Rosemary too reckless? Or was this a mark of her regard for Florence?

I cannot tell you how I look forward to the next instalment of Carmilla's adventures. I so look forward to Miss Hancock's escape —and to hear all your news, rabbit! It is so typical of you to say nothing of yourself. How do you get on with the Temples? Are you happy? Do they treat you well? What sort of woman is Mrs Temple? Is she the warrior she appeared in the photo or a different sort altogether? I am afire to hear more.

Julian wishes to know if his map was useful, and Basil sends his regards. I remain,

Your dear friend,

Rosemary Scott.

Friend!

Florence looked a long time at that word, her misgivings undone. Rosemary thought her a friend!

Mr Temple looked up at the breakfast table. "You look radiant this morning, Miss Skelton. Good news from home? Or a letter from your sweetheart?"

Florence blushed and shook her head as she sat. "A letter from a friend. It is good to know one is thought of."

"Miss Skelton must be well thought of wherever she goes," Mr Temple said.

Florence never knew how to react to such compliments. She reached for the teapot. "You do not have a cup of tea, Mr Temple, Mr Vaugham. Shall I pour?"

Mr Temple inclined his head. "Please."

"No tea for me. I much prefer coffee." Mr Vaugham set down the letter he'd been reading with a combative air.

"No tea?" Mr Temple repeated. "And India famous for it! Where is your national pride?"

"I have none," Mr Vaugham said. "How can I be proud of a country I barely know?"

"Country is more than location," Mr Temple insisted. "I should be an Englishman no matter where in the world I was. My language, my culture—"

"That is your privilege," Mr Vaugham cut in. "I was raised

outside my birth culture, educated at an English school, by my adopted father. I did not even know my parents. When I returned to India as a man, it was to a place unknown and unfamiliar."

"You are a child of the Empire," Mr Temple started. "As such—" His lecture was an adaptation of his favourite theme: the elevating properties of education.

Florence saw mutiny glitter in Mr Vaugham's eyes. She set his cup in front of him. "Your coffee, Mr Vaugham."

Mr Temple frowned as Florence placed his cup in front of him. "You're not joining me, Miss Skelton?"

"I think that today I shall try Mr Vaugham's example and start my day with coffee." Florence poured herself a cup from the coffee tureen.

"The Englishman starts his day with tea." Mr Temple slapped the table. "The custom not only unites us, but the civilising properties of tea—"

Florence wilted. She'd hoped to take the edge off Mr Temple's bad humour with her action, not exacerbate it. Now she had not only angered her employer, but she was stuck with a cup of unpalatable coffee.

Mr Vaugham's wry expression indicated he grasped her dilemma. He pushed the tray of cream and sugar across the table.

Even this attracted Mr Temple's ire. "It says much that coffee cannot be drunk unadulterated, whereas tea is drinkable with or without milk or sugar. Tea therefore is the superior beverage."

Mr Vaugham bowed his head. "I understand the Chinese regard the English custom of adding milk as an act of savagery."

Mr Temple glared at him. "I have much work to do. I shall drink my tea in the study. Miss Skelton, I shall expect you at nine. Vaugham, you can start on the dig."

"Please excuse me," Florence said, once Mr Temple had vacated the breakfast table. "I did not mean to provoke him."

"I did." Vaugham grimaced. "It is too easy to rile him these days."

Florence hesitated. "Does it seem to you that Mr Temple's temper is growing worse? I don't wish to speak ill of him, but I do not know if it is my imagination or…"

"He's under a lot of pressure to make another find." Mr Vaugham gulped his coffee. "We've had several letters from sponsors wanting to know how our work progresses. They don't realise how hard it is to work in the rain. No sooner do we drain our excavation trench, it fills up again."

Florence nodded. Bad weather had confined Temple and Vaugham to the house for days. "You cannot put off your excavations until the summer?"

"If only! No, the sponsors want their money's worth and they will not wait until the weather clears." Vaugham drained the last of his coffee. "No rest for the wicked, as they say."

Florence sat down at her desk in the study with trepidation, but Mr Temple seemed occupied with a study of his ordinance maps. He muttered to himself, tracing the locations of previous finds and marking out where they'd already excavated.

Florence set to work.

She fancied she was making excellent progress. Her proficiency with the typewriter had increased. Mr Temple seemed pleased with her speed, and she had already completed one year's worth of notes. As Florence progressed through her current notebook, a paragraph caught her attention.

Mrs Rutherford joined us today and should suit us admirably. She comes to us from the society for abandoned women. Not an orphan, as I had understood, but she tells me her family does not care whether she lives or dies. She married against their wishes, it seems, and the subsequent desertion of her husband before his death

Florence's fingers moved automatically, her mind turning over the words. Was Mrs Rutherford the secretary before Florence? Neither Mr Temple nor his wife had spoken of her, and Mr Vaugham had only arrived a few months before Florence.

How cruel—to be cut off from one's family for the choice of whom one married… Florence pressed her lips together. Her parents would just be pleased to have her married and off their hands! She must give Mr Temple no reason to complain of her work. Having tasted such freedom as Aylesport offered, the thought of returning to her father's rigid discipline was unpalatable in the extreme.

Florence did not wish to contemplate that. Instead, her thoughts drifted to a more agreeable dilemma: what to do with Carmilla. She had, through clever contriving, set herself up with a school and saved enough that Miss Hancock had joined her and taught the junior pupils. Their enterprise had attracted some resistance from the madame principal of a finishing school who accused them of making their young ladies unmarriageable. Through a fortunate encounter with the principal of a nearby boy's school whom Carmilla had plucked from a flooded river, they made ends meet. Now, however, Carmilla's grasping guardian was hot on their trail —and with him, Lord Hancock, almost as great a villain as Baron Crump.

Florence was still puzzling over how to extricate Carmilla from this predicament when she set out for her afternoon walk. She was alone, Mrs Temple, occupied with household matters, granting her permission to walk alone provided she stay within the bounds of Old House.

The usual ending to any story was a marriage—and the principal was a good man. But was he worthy of Carmilla? Florence hesitated. Married, Carmilla's property would be her husband's, and neither her guardian, Baron Crump, nor Lord Hancock would have any claim on her. The solution was easy… And yet, it was not right.

A shiver ran through her body. She'd been standing still so long the damp grass had seeped into her dress. She shook out her skirts, turning back towards the house.

The weather had turned. Mist drifted in over the bogs. The thick cloud reduced Old House to an ominous shape in the distance, and the path was indistinct.

If she didn't return now, she would lose the path. Florence stepped towards the house and stopped dead.

A woman wearing a dark dress walked out of the dairy. She paused, looking towards the house, and then walked on. She did not follow the path. Instead, she made for the boathouse.

Florence's skin crawled as she stared after the woman. She did not have Margot's way of walking, and she was too tall to be the cook. At this distance she could not be sure, but she was certain she'd seen this woman before—ankle-deep in Foxwood Pond.

It was not the shock it should have been. Florence had felt those cold fingers around her neck in her dreams, heard her voice in the trickle of the rain in the gutters.

The woman continued to walk. In another moment, she would be lost in the mist. Florence gathered her skirts, preparing to run. She could be back at the house within seconds.

Rosemary wouldn't run.

Florence dug her fingers into her skirts. She wasn't Rosemary. But if she wanted to be worthy of Rosemary's attention, she could not let this chance go.

What to do? Florence dared not take her gaze from the woman, fast disappearing in the fog. Another moment and she would be lost entirely—

Rosemary would not hesitate.

Borrowed courage propelled her forward. Florence stepped off the path onto the grass.

The woman did not believe any would follow her—she did not so much as glance behind. Her shoulders sloped forward, as if weighed down by thought. She passed the boathouse, striking out into the bog. Her skirts were quickly soaked, but she maintained an even pace, climbing out of the bog onto a rise.

Florence's heart quailed at the thought of stepping into the water. The surface was as clouded as the sky above and it was hard to tell where land ended and marsh began.

She might not have this chance again. Florence bunched up her skirts and took a running leap for the clump of grass.

There was no sign of the woman, but Florence heard splashes ahead. She jogged after her, only to come up against the water.

Florence scanned the bank but did not see any way across.

She had reached a dead end.

Splashing water caught her attention. Florence stepped backwards.

Ahead of her the woman walked straight ahead. The water was already at her shoulders, but she showed no sign of stopping. As Florence stared, the water closed over her head, ripples fading into nothingness.

Gone.

17

Florence's legs gave way. She folded onto the moss, skirts ballooning out around her. Her mind fought against what she'd seen: a woman walking to her death.

I must help. Do something—

Florence's limbs did not obey her. She could not seem to regain her feet. "Help—please! Someone, hear me!"

The swirling mist and the distant ripple of water was the only response. Florence choked on a sob. No one was coming to her aid.

Her legs still shook, but by pitching herself forward, she could lever herself upright. She lurched to the water.

There were no bubbles, not even a ripple. Nothing now to show the woman had ever existed at all.

Am I going mad? Florence pressed her hands to her mouth, holding back a moan. Fear threatened to drag her under.

Her mother's words echoed in her head; *A young lady is always in command of herself.* Florence dug her nails into her palms until her breathing evened out. She staggered forward.

Was this the way? The mist swirled, melting away at her approach. The grass took on a sameness in the half-light.

A light flickered. Old House! Florence gasped in relief. She could follow the light.

The grass sagged beneath her next step, giving way. Florence waded through the water. It was deeper than she remembered. She needed both hands to pull herself up the bank. Reeds snagged her skirts, threatening to drag her back down. Florence tugged herself free, almost losing a boot.

She righted herself—and stared. Two lights flickered in the marsh. As she watched, one faded from view. The remaining light hovered in the mist, then floated away.

The will-o'-the-wisp. Florence pressed her hands to her mouth. *Ignis Fatuus.* Marsh gas burned, creating phantom lights to lead unwary travellers astray. She was lost.

Florence sat on the grassy outcrop. She did not know how long she'd been sitting there when she heard the even and repetitive ripple of something moving through the water. It took a moment to register. Her mind had passed through fear to resignation—she was not brave enough to wrestle again with the swamp. She must stay and pray for rescue. Anything else was beyond her.

Was this rescue? Florence parted the reeds to peer into the fog.

She saw nothing, but a feminine voice travelled to her on the breeze. "I swear I smelled someone…"

"In this stinking bog?" another woman answered. "You're imagining things."

Florence shrank back with a whimper. She did not want to be dragged into the bog, feel the water flooding her throat and nose, her lungs. Her hand crept over her mouth, as if she might protect herself…

The rhythmic swish of water tugged at her memory. The

woman from the pond had sunk into the bog without a ripple. This—this was a boat!

And if it was a boat—

Florence staggered to her feet. "Hello! Hello there!"

A lantern flashed, dazzling her with its brightness. Florence blinked, her eyes adjusting to reveal a completely unexpected sight.

Two young women not more than a handful of years older than Florence and dressed in smart blouses, practical skirts, and tailored jackets exchanged a glance. The woman holding the oars manoeuvred the boat around. Her friend—stout, with a scattering of ginger curls and a large helping of freckles—stood.

"Hello there. I don't wish to make assumptions, especially considering that we have not yet been introduced, but judging from your attire and location in the bog, are we to infer that—"

"Brevity, Jemina," muttered the other woman, bringing the dinghy alongside Florence's knoll.

Her companion did not pause. "—you are in need of some assistance effecting your removal from said bog?"

Florence could have wept. "Your inference is correct."

The rower held out a hand. "Climb aboard."

Florence scrambled into the boat. "I'm at Old House—do you know it? They'll have noticed I'm gone and be worried."

The rower squinted at the cloud surrounding them. "I don't know if I'd care to risk the swamp at this late hour. We'd be rowing in circles."

"Brick knows the way," the curly-haired woman asserted. "She'll have our guest home in two flicks of a tail, doncha know." She beamed at Florence. "You do not object to coming home with us?"

Florence felt miles better already. "In the circumstances, I should be glad. Where is home?"

"We're renting two old cottages yonder," Jemima waved a

hand at the fog. "Or is it over there? This is why Pat is in charge of the oars."

Pat did not seem perturbed by the fog. "Introduce us."

"Where are my manners? Excuse me." Jemima's curls bounced as she shook her head. "Allow me to present the Honourable Patricia Fenley, rower and navigator extraordinaire. I am the dishonourable Jemima Barr, amateur photographer. And you, our fair guest, are a lady in distress, fleeing the demands of some wretched suitor?"

Her parents would have disapproved of Jemima and her loose way of talking, but Florence found her chatter comforting. "I'm afraid I simply got lost."

"Didn't anyone tell you about the dangers of the bog? Shocking neglect, if so."

"I knew. I—" Florence gasped, the horror of the situation coming back to her. "There was a woman. I followed her. She walked straight into the bog."

Jemima and Pat exchanged a glance. "A woman, you say? Black haired, pale, sort of wet-looking?"

"Yes, but I don't think you understand. She walked into the bog—right into it!" Florence started to stand. The boat rocked.

"Easy there!" Pat clutched the oars and Jemima flung out a hand to Florence.

"Careful now. I'm in no hurry to take a swim."

"But the woman—"

"If you saw who I think you saw," Pat said, continuing to draw the boat through the water, "then she was not the one in danger. You've had a lucky escape, Miss Skelton."

Florence blinked. "You know my name."

"There's only so many young women in this vicinity—besides ourselves, I mean," Jemima said. "The stationmaster mentioned you. Matter of fact, we were wishing to make your acquaintance, lurking round the village in the hopes we might run into you doing your shopping, but so far, no joy."

"Mr Temple worries about my reputation should I go out alone. I don't leave Old House."

Significant looks seemed to be a speciality of her companions. They exchanged another. "Well, we're acquainted now," Pat said. "And about to be better acquainted." She navigated around a slight hillock, revealing a row of lanterns that lead the way to a small dock. Two stone cottages sharing one wall were visible beyond, as were two more female figures, standing at the dock.

"Brick," Jemima nodded towards a short, stout woman, whose pince-nez did not disguise an alert, eager gaze. "And Jackie." Jackie wore the same uniform of a jacket, blouse, and practical skirts, but had switched out the bonnet for an engineer's cap. She whistled in surprise as the boat drew near.

"If I'd know we were expecting company, I'd have made something more exciting than soup." She held out a hand to assist Florence ashore. Her grip was strong.

Florence had never been happier to be on dry ground. "I couldn't intrude. I've already been enough of a bother."

"Miss Skelton encountered the bog lady," Pat reported.

"Which takes you out of the category of bothers and puts you somewhere in the ranks of honoured guest." Jemima leaped to shore with a confidence that astonished Florence. "Come on."

Jemima ushered Florence into the first cottage where she discovered a large fire, a pot of soup on the stove, and more crinolines and petticoats than she could count. Florence stopped in the doorway in shock. She'd never been confronted with so many undergarments in her life.

Jemima collided with her back, propelling Florence inside. She turned in confusion, intending to make her escape, but Brick and Jackie were coming inside behind her.

"Stand by the fire," Jemima suggested. "Let's see what we can do about your skirts."

"I can't," Florence protested. "I mean—"

"We're all women here." Brick said. "It's nothing we haven't seen."

They persuaded Florence to remove her dress so it could dry next to the kitchen stove while she stood in her petticoats next to the fire.

Jemima stoked the embers. "I expect that you're wondering what four such exceptional young ladies such as ourselves are doing out here in the middle of a bog. We're lepidopterists, which, in case you don't know, is the—"

"Study of moths and butterflies." Florence tucked a stray curl behind her ear.

Jackie looked up from the peat she was piling on the fire, and Brick looked up from her notebook. Even Pat and Jemima gave her an appraising stare. "Are you a lepidopterist yourself?"

Florence's heart gave a sudden lurch. She forced herself to smile. "No, no. I just—I have heard of it."

She dug her fingers into the fabric of dress, trying to supress her sudden alarm. It had not been apparent outside, but in the better lighting of the cottage, she saw that all four women had identical amber-coloured eyes.

18

"Perhaps you don't realise it, Miss Skelton, given how much of the jolly marsh there is around here, but a swamp like this is rather rare." Brick, the oldest of the four women, assumed the role of lecturer. "It provides a habitat for many forms of insect life that one would not find elsewhere. We propose to make an in-depth study of the moths and butterflies of this locale and are hot on the trail of a rare species, described in the writings of a seventeenth century scientist and not seen since."

Florence nodded, sipping the bowl of soup Jackie had provided her. It was homely fare, the sort her mother would have made for the deserving poor, and exactly what she needed after her experience in the swamp. "And that is why you are here?" She hesitated. How was she to phrase this? "Is this your entire party?"

"That it is," Jemima beamed. "Jackie chops our wood and is in charge of the food. Brick organises our search for the mystery moth and maps our search. Pat is the navigator and secures our groceries, and I oversee morale and housework."

"Morale." Jackie raised her eyebrows. "Is that what you call it?"

Florence interrupted before the two could get side-tracked. "And your menfolk?"

Again, a look passed across the four women. "We do fine without."

"But—"

"We're committed spinsters," Jemima explained. "We share a medical condition that prevents us from marriage. Can't risk handing it on, doncha know."

A medical condition—did that explain their unusual eye colour? "I am so sorry—" Florence began.

Pat shook her head. "Don't be."

"Our numbers are few," Brick said, "but there are enough of us we have banded together to form a mutual support society, while our common interest in Lepidoptera gives us purpose."

A society of women? Her father would never approve. And yet… Florence cast a look around the cottage. Aside from the profusion of petticoats, the cottage was unremarkable. If this was a den of iniquity, it was a very well kept one. "So that is why you're in Aylesport. I can't imagine why I did not hear of you."

"We keep to ourselves," Jackie said. "Most people hear of a gathering of women and assume the worst."

Florence blushed. "Do you think you can find your way to Old House in these conditions? I don't like to think of them searching for me in this weather."

"Once you're warmed and have eaten, I'll be happy to take you," Brick assured her. "I have trails of my own to follow. Not to mention, I would be glad to meet Mr Temple. It is because of him we can search for this moth at all."

Florence tilted her head. "I was not aware that Mr Temple had an interest in Lepidoptera." He seemed to think of only archaeology.

"He has no idea of how we're indebted to him," Brick continued. "A scheme was proposed to convert the swamp to farmland. The village opposed it, but they were overruled. The bogs were on the brink of being lost when Mr Temple made his great find."

"You mean, Mrs Temple made *her* great find," Pat cut in.

"Mrs Temple—not that she was Mrs Temple at the time—took an object she'd found in the bog to the curate, knowing his interest in the area's history. Mr Temple recognised the object's value and significance and discovered several more objects. On the strength of his arguments, the scheme was postponed, and the bog preserved so he might continue his archaeological expeditions."

Florence frowned. "Postponed—not abandoned?"

"It comes up for debate again in a few months," Jackie said. "Meaning we have little time to find our moth."

"And Mr Temple a find worth preserving the bog for." Brick put her bowl of soup down. "Are you ready to depart, Miss Skelton?"

Florence stood with some reluctance. Exchanging the warmth of the cottage for damp skirts and the uncertainty of the bog was a poor bargain, but she had to return to Old House.

Holding a lantern aloft, Brick led the way along the path with a confidence that Florence could only marvel at. "I could navigate these swamps in the dark, I've been over them so often."

Florence gathered her courage. "The dark-haired lady I saw in the swamp—is she a member of your party?"

Brick turned to glance at her. "No. She is not."

"Jemima referred to her as 'the bog lady.'" Florence swallowed. "Is she known to you?"

Brick seemed to give the matter some thought. "Only by reputation—if a legend can possess a reputation."

"A legend?"

"The very nature of the marshes gives rise to legends. The will-o'-the-wisp, the not infrequent cases of travellers becoming lost or drowning… In addition to sightings of the marsh gas, people claim to have seen people walking where no live person could walk, heard voices speaking in unknown languages, even seen those known to have drowned decades earlier." Brick resumed her steady pace. "The path is muddy here. Mind you don't slip."

Florence navigated around a puddle. "How is that possible?"

"One theory is that the marsh gas addles the minds of those lost in the swamp, producing hallucinations. Those lost would already be in a nervous condition, their minds ripe for such an illusion."

But Florence had seen the woman even before she'd ventured off the path and into the swamp. She hesitated, only to notice a light up ahead. "Old House!"

Brick polished her pince-nez. "Didn't I tell you I knew the way?"

The Temples and Mr Vaugham were very pleased to see her, the coats drying by the fire proving their claim of only just having called off their search.

"We knew Miss Skelton was too sensible to venture far once she'd realised she had left the path," Mr Temple explained, once he'd ascertained Florence was well and settled her before the fireplace. "We planned to resume our search once it grew light enough." He bowed to Brick. "We owe you a great deal of thanks for returning our lost sheep, Miss Brickwell."

"It was my great pleasure to do you a favour," Brick replied. "You've done us a great service with your work, Mr Temple."

Mr Temple tugged his moustache with a flattered air. "I am gratified you think so. Are you familiar with archaeology?"

"I am acquainted with it via your secretary, Mrs Rutherford, though I have not heard from her of late." Miss Brickwell glanced around, as if noticing for the first time that Mrs Temple and Florence were the only women in the room. "Is she still with you?"

Mr Temple gaped. He darted a glance at his wife, then turned his most disarming grin on Brick. "Mrs Rutherford left us some years ago. She did not inform us of her destination, I am afraid."

"Such a pity," Brick murmured. "It seems to have been a while since any have heard from Mrs Rutherford." She turned, giving Florence a small nod. "I have enjoyed making your acquaintance, Miss Skelton. Now you know where we are you must come and visit us again."

"I should be delighted." Florence squeezed Brick's hand. "Thank you for everything, Miss Brickwell."

Brick took her leave, and Florence muffled a yawn. She was more than ready for her bed.

"A very officious woman. Who is she, Miss Skelton? How did you come to be acquainted?" Mr Temple demanded.

Florence retold the story of being found and rescued by the lepidopterists, though she left out certain elements. She omitted seeing the woman and what Brick had told her of Mr Temple's actions. She did not need Mr Vaugham's warnings to know that Mr Temple would not appreciate the reminder that his reputation rested on his claims that Aylesport bog concealed a major archaeological find.

Mr Temple made her repeat her story three times before he was satisfied. "Lepidopterists," he snorted. "Ridiculous. What these women need is a husband and a child to occupy themselves. This is the danger of single women. They need supervision!"

"And those unable to marry?" Mr Vaugham could never pass up an opportunity to question his employer.

"They have fathers, don't they? And brothers?"

A complete reversal of the conversation Mr Temple had on the subject with Florence's father.

Her spirits sank. "If you do not mind, I shall retire. I am exhausted."

But it wasn't only Mr Temple's mutable opinion that worried her. As Florence undressed for bed, the strangeness of Miss Brickwell's question occurred to her. Brick had known that Florence was Mr Temple's secretary. Why the interest in Mrs Rutherford?

19

The week following Florence's sighting of the pond woman was miserable and misty. There was only bright spot: a letter from Rosemary.

Carmilla's reunion with Miss Hancock was everything I wished. Your depiction of their friendship gives me such joy—you clever thing! Such an example of feminine solidarity will inspire and uplift young women everywhere.

Florence's heard sank. Surely, Rosemary did not imagine that Florence intended to publish her work? She scanned the rest of the letter.

I beg you will not marry Carmilla to the principal. It makes sense from a publishing perspective—society considers only one potential career for a woman—but to relegate so bright a star as Carmilla to mere helpmeet seems cruel beyond words.

That was the problem, wasn't it? Florence had no thought of winning a publisher's approval, but to come up with an ending that would satisfy Rosemary… It was a test Florence wasn't sure her imagination was equal to.

That night she settled down with her notebook. The words that had come so easily now eluded her. Carmilla refused the principal's proposal, citing a need to keep her independence. Rather than remain where she knew she might cause pain to him, she set off again, in search of fresh challenges. Rosemary was sure to approve.

But as Florence moved downstairs to type up the pages to send them off the following morning, she couldn't help but feel flat.

"This miserable weather!" To add to her problems, her dreams had gotten worse. When she shut her eyes the mist was always before her, and the murky echo of the water never far away. Getting up from the desk, Florence walked over to the bookshelf. She counted the remaining books of field notes, calculating how many months it would take her to complete her work. Far too long.

She'd had enough of typing. Florence tugged the pages from the typewriter and climbed the stairs to her room. But even as she lay in bed, her thoughts could not settle. Marriage to the principal would end Carmilla's story—but Florence dreaded consigning her to the isolation demanded by her independent spirit. For all her strength, Carmilla needed a tempering influence, a companion—an equal.

Florence caught her breath. If Carmilla refused the principal—only to have him prove himself worthy of her by respecting her independence, nay, by supporting her in her work...

Could it work? Florence sat up, reaching for her notebook. Her candle burned out before she'd committed her thoughts to paper.

With a sigh, Florence closed her notebook and shut her eyes. Carmilla sprung to life before them. Her mind retraced the words she'd written and those yet to come.

The next morning, Florence flew through her work, eager to return to her story. Carmilla and her refusal seemed more real to her than the field notes and the endless record of the dig.

As she finished one book of field notes and lifted out the

next, a few pages of notepaper dropped to the floor. Florence unfolded the pages. They were in Mr Temple's handwriting and stained with something that left them tacky. Were they connected to his work?

The Canopic jars contain the viscera, while the body embalmed with natron (salt) and oils. Worth looking into. The reports from Denmark describe discolouration of the skin, and decay where parts of the body were exposed to the air. The internal organs do not appear to have survived, nor did the clothing. Signs of violent death—strangulation.

Florence frowned. There was a big shift between field notes, and notes on... She tilted her head, re-reading the notes... embalming? Then again, reports from Denmark might refer to the bog body found there.

Florence set the paper aside and returned to her typing.

Nothing in the notes had any bearing on the piece of paper. When Florence heard the clutter of boots and coats being removed that heralded Mr Temple and Mr Vaugham's return, she went out into the hallway. "Mr Temple, might I trouble you for a moment?"

Mr Temple beamed. The previous day they'd found some shards of pottery, and from his good humour, it appeared they'd uncovered some more. "How may I assist, Miss Skelton?"

"I started on a new notebook and some loose papers fell out. I was hoping you could tell me if they are connected to your work."

Mr Temple glanced over the pages and the good humour vanished from his face. His jaw clenched, skin blanching a fierce white. "What are you doing with these?"

Florence scuttled backwards. "They fell out of the notebook."

Mr Temple picked up the notebook, glancing through it. With effort, he unclenched his jaw. "You did not type them up?"

"No." Florence twisted her hands in the neck of her dress. "I wanted to consult you first."

Mr Temple's grimace looked forced; a grotesque parody of a smile. "You did the right thing. As you no doubt discerned, these were notes on a paper I was reviewing, unconnected with my research." He tucked the paper in his pocket, picking up the notebook. "This is what you are working on now?"

Florence nodded.

"Well, you've made remarkable progress, Miss Skelton. I think this calls for some recognition—the rest of the morning is yours to spend as you would wish."

"That's very kind of you, Mr Temple." Florence dropped a quick curtsey and hurried from the study, her heart pounding. Escape from Mr Temple's variable tempers was welcome.

At lunch, Mr Temple suggested that Mr Vaugham take Florence for a walk to show her the dig. "It would no doubt benefit Miss Temple to see how we go about our work."

Florence professed herself curious, and Mr Vaugham was not sorry to put aside work to show off their progress. He demonstrated the pump used to remove water from their working trench, and how they sifted through the peat for artefacts. He uncovered more pottery shards in the process, and they returned to Old House eager to share this news with Mr Temple.

They found Mr Temple in the study, stoking the fire. He was pleased with their news, but Florence thought him a trifle preoccupied.

"I am very grateful to Mr Vaugham for the demonstration, and to you for the suggestion," she said. "He has put many of my notions regarding archaeology straight."

"Very pleased to hear it, my dear." Mr Temple motioned her from the room. "Why don't you retire and leave me and Vaugham to discuss these new finds."

Florence was in no mood to get caught in another argument between the two men. She wasted no time returning to her room. Her heart thrilled with anticipation as she opened her notebook and took up her pen, picking up where she'd left off: Carmilla's refusal of the principal's proposal. *"There is no man that I regard with more respect than you. And yet, to accept your proposal would be to destroy the friendship I hold so dear. Where there is not equality, there cannot be genuine love, and where both parties are not equal, resentment must grow and poison love."*

The words flowed. Florence wrote as she had not written in days—it was a challenge for her pen to keep up with the words flowing from her mind. She did not hear the dinner bell, so absorbed was she in her task. In fact, it was not until she had penned the last words that she emerged from Carmilla's world.

With the story complete, Florence felt both pleased with herself and flat—a feeling that lasted to the following morning. How was she to occupy her time now? Sitting once again at the typewriter, working on Mr Temple's notes, she heaved a sigh so loud, she startled herself.

This was no time to become morbid. Florence stood, walking over to the fireplace to poke the fire. A few scraps escaped the grate.

Was that—note paper? The scraps were scorched, but she thought she recognised Mr Temple's writing. Florence walked back to her desk, flicking back through the pages of the notebook she'd been typing.

It was— whole pages had been torn from the field notebook!

Florence stood still. Why on earth would Mr Temple want to destroy his work? As Mr Vaugham so often stated, a historian must be as accurate as possible. How could he be accurate without keeping accurate records?

ow clever you are, rabbit! You have done justice to Carmilla's proud and independent spirit and done it in such a way that even the most scurrilous of moralists has nothing to complain about. She must marry, if only to satisfy convention— you will reach more readers that way. But in showing an equal partnership, a veritable meeting of minds, you may light the spark of change, even while obeying society's dictates.

Rosemary's letters were the high point of Florence's life at Aylesport. Her confidences thrilled, and her comments on Carmilla delighted Florence, even as they alarmed her. Reach more readers... She'd told Rosemary she didn't intend to publish.

The fire crackled, the bright coals sending a gentle glow throughout the room. Florence pulled her chair closer to the fire, balancing her candleholder on the arm of the chair to read.

It has been such a relief to turn to Carmilla and to you. Life here grows more unendurable by the day. I took your book and an apple into the woods, intending to have an afternoon to myself. I came home to find a search party assembled. Honestly! Julian can disappear for an entire day and no one minds, but a young woman

—a capable young woman—cannot even have a few hours of privacy. It is worse than (the next words were scribbled out). I feel like the only place I have where I can have any solitude is my mind.

One of the ridiculous old women who live in the village has complained to Lord Cross that I set a poor example walking by myself. Who could object to someone walking? I make it a point now to pass her house whenever I go for a ramble.

Florence's heart sank. Worse and worse. Rosemary's soul craved independence, but her actions could only bring her further censure—and greater restraint. She picked up her pen.

Foxwood is a small village, and the occupants take a great deal of interest in each other's lives. A minor matter may take on great significance. I beg that, rather than provoke the displeasure of our neighbours, you adopt a more usual manner of doing things, at least until you are better known. It is not merely your reputation at stake, but your brother's. A tutor living with the family as he does must be above reproach. Should Mr Scott desire to open a school of his own, the reputation, not just of him but of his family, is of even more importance.

She paused, reviewing her words. Would Rosemary take her meaning without offence? This was as hard to write as ending the manuscript had been.

In your letter you mentioned readers. This is impossible. I have told you how my father would object to his daughter becoming an author. It is enough for me you have enjoyed my work. I should like it to remain our secret.

Florence breathed out. Rosemary could not object to that, could she?

I remain your devoted friend,
Florence Skelton.

She looked at the letter for many minutes. A sudden gust of wind shook the shutters over Florence's windows. The violent rattle startled Florence, her hand flying to her throat.

She felt again the icy fingers of the pond woman around her neck.

Unbidden, the image of shrivelled white fingers clasped around a candle sprang into her mind. Florence shuddered, pushing the memory of the Hand of Glory from her mind. A thought rose in its wake.

P.S. When Mr Temple visited Foxwood Court, did he talk to Mr Leighton about embalming?

She handed her letter to Graham to post and took her usual place at the typewriter, knowing that she would not have a moment's peace until she got Rosemary's reply.

Weeks went past without a return letter from Foxwood. Had she so offended Rosemary that she'd decided not to reply?

More likely, Rosemary had found a friend better suited to her. Florence knew herself too meek and ordinary to have any claim to Rosemary's attention for long—and with Carmilla's story concluded, what interest did she hold for someone so full of life and energy? The only surprising thing about this was that it had taken so long for Rosemary to tire of her.

Florence re-counted the remaining notebooks, calculating when she might return to Foxwood. Would it be better to be in Rosemary's vicinity, even without her company? Or would the occasional glimpse of her be more painful than this current neglect?

Florence had so reconciled herself to the loss of their friendship that when the envelope arrived for her she did not recognise Rosemary's handwriting.

Forgive the long silence, rabbit. I was waiting until I had news for you—and now I do! Let me be the first to congratulate you on Carmilla's publication.

Had she misread? Florence moved her candle closer to the letter. No—the words remained just as she'd seen them.

"Publication." Her mouth tasted of curdled milk. What did Rosemary mean? There was another piece of paper enclosed, typed on stiff paper and bearing the letterhead of a London publishing house.

Dear Miss Skelton,

We must congratulate you on so masterful a debut novel. Although in need of some polishing, the quality of your work is clear, and your commitment to the truth of a young woman's desire for freedom and her right to determine her own happiness admirable. Clytemnestra Press is pleased to accept Carmilla for publication.

"No," Florence whispered. "Oh no." Her father would be furious! He would not allow her to return home—to return even to Foxwood. She would be an outcast, and, once her work with the Temples finished, she would be alone.

The papers slipped from her trembling fingers. She knelt to gather them—Rosemary's letter was foremost.

The terms are reasonable. I asked Mr Leighton, and he says that an advance of 100 pounds is usual. Once the book has paid back the advance, you will receive royalties quarterly. But more than the royalties is the knowledge that your work will reach hundreds, nay, thousands of young women, inspiring them to find courage of their own.

I know you protested that you could not publish, but I know that was just your modesty talking. There is nothing to prevent you from adopting a pseudonym. In fact, it seems to be usual in the publishing world. Your family need never know and having an income of your own would allow you to become even further independent.

Florence's heart sank further. How had Rosemary misunderstood her so completely? No—this wasn't a case of misunderstanding. This was far, far worse.

Florence sank into her chair. She had to blink back tears to even see the paper as she wrote.

You must write to Clytemnestra Press and refuse their offer. It was not modesty that prevents me from publishing, but my sense of duty. I do not think you realise how deep my father's objection would go, or how repugnant it is to me to contemplate a pseudonym. If I cannot do a thing under my name, then I will not do it at all.

A tear ran down her cheek, threatening to spill onto the paper. Florence wiped her face with the sleeve of her dress. More even than the threat of publishing was the sting of this betrayal.

I told you that I did not wish to publish, and you ignored my wishes and contacted a publisher. This is not the act of a friend. You had no right to ignore my decision. What you propose would put a divide between myself and my family that would take years to repair—if repair would be possible at all.

Finally, you spoke of my book inspiring others. You must see how unfit I am to teach anyone. I am not educated. I struggle even to teach the village children their Sunday lesson. Holding my work up as a model for young minds is not just impossible, it is unwise! I cannot be responsible for the consequences, I just cannot.

Florence dispatched her letter the next day. This time the reply came within days. Rosemary was displeased, her handwriting large and scrawling across the page.

This is no time to get scared! To keep Carmilla from the public is a crime. The story must be shared as widely as possible. To protest that your family would disapprove is absurd. What is one man's opinion compared to the potential of your story to free so many women from despondent servitude? I have long thought your family does not value you as they ought. Why should they then control you as they do? If the bond between you is so weak to be severed by your publishing, then such a bond does not deserve your care at all. You are not so much of a coward, are you?

Florence's heart sank. Rosemary would not apologise or back down. There was only one option.

If it is cowardly to care about the consequences of one's actions on those one cares about, then yes, I am a coward. I do not want to risk my father's livelihood, nor the wellbeing of the rest of my family. You ignored my stated wishes, pursuing your own agenda.

Florence's hand shook. She took a deep breath before taking up her pen again.

Where there is no trust, no equality, there can be no friendship. If you cannot respect my decision, then it is for the best that we no longer correspond.

To cut herself off from Rosemary's letters was more than her heart could bear. But there was no other way. She had exerted no influence over Rosemary, only been led into an action she knew her family could never condone.

I will treasure the time we spent together and the many happy hours your letters have given. I hope you will not think of me too harshly.

Yours,

Florence.

She sat for many minutes, simply looking at the envelope. Finally, with a sigh, she reached forward and extinguished the candle. This was the end.

21

If the Temples noticed their secretary was downcast and no longer looked forward to the mail's arrival, they were too tactful to comment on it. More likely, their own concerns preoccupied them. Mr Temple was preparing a report for his sponsors and often interrupted Florence's typing to ask where certain records were, or to request that she type up a letter for him. From the fervour with which he insisted that he was on the trail of something grand, Florence inferred that his sponsors were growing impatient.

Mrs Temple remained as she always had—calm, serene, removed. She spent more time in silent contemplation than she did knitting, and often left Florence at the house, preferring to walk in solitude. Even Mr Vaugham felt the increased tension, ceasing to needle Mr Temple.

No reply came from Rosemary. Florence could only imagine that she had taken her at her word.

Florence lay awake long into the night, her thoughts travelling on a by now familiar journey. She should not have cared so much. A friendship so easily severed was not a real friendship, and yet no one had ever understood her as Rosemary understood her. How, then, had she misjudged Florence so much? Or was Florence at fault, and Rosemary right? No—Florence could never inspire others as Rosemary claimed. She had allowed her enthusiasm to run riot. That was all.

But a publisher had praised the book…

She would not get any sleep like this. Florence lit her candle, and, wrapping herself in her shawl, made her way downstairs. She could take one of Mr Temple's many volumes of history and read that until she felt sleepy.

Florence set down the candle and perused the shelves. As she did, a light from outside caught her attention.

A will-o'-the-wisp? Florence shrank back, then caught herself. Was she always to be a coward? She was inside, protected from the marsh by sturdy stone walls. There was nothing to fear.

She peeped out from between the curtains. Instead of the dancing flame she expected, she saw the bright yellow glow of a lantern. The tread of boots accompanied it. Mr Temple strode right past the house, making his way towards Mr Vaugham's cottage.

Florence stayed motionless. The household had retired to bed many hours ago, and Mr Temple had ample time to talk to Mr Vaugham at their work. Why was he calling on the student so late at night? And where had Mr Temple come from? She had not heard him leave the house.

Whatever was happening, it did not concern her. Florence took a volume at random from the bookshelf and returned to her room. Yet, she could not concentrate on the survey of Roman Britain. Her mind kept puzzling over Mr Temple's unaccountable behaviour.

A few minutes after she'd retired a second time, Florence heard a door close, and furtive steps tracking along the corridor. She opened her door a crack, just enough to see Mr Temple slip into his bedroom.

She shut her door with a sigh. Now that everyone was where they should be, maybe she could get some sleep.

But Florence received no rest that night. No sooner had she lain down then a sudden thud called her attention to her window. Was someone there?

Absurd—she was on the second floor!

The sound repeated. Florence drew back the curtains and leaned out. "Who's there?"

"Miss Skelton." Mr Vaugham's voice. "Thank God you're awake. I know this is inappropriate, but I need help."

What on earth was going on? "Are you injured? Ill? I will inform Mr Temple—"

"No—no! Please, not a word to the Temples. Come to the study window—I'll tell you everything."

Her father would not have approved. Her mother would have been aghast. Hannah—what Hannah would think was better not contemplated. Florence threw a shawl around her shoulders and hurried downstairs.

Mr Vaugham had no light. He was a shadow against the window glass, turning as Florence threw open the window-pane. His clothing was soaked, water running off him in rivulets.

"You are wet through! What happened?"

"What I am about to tell you will sound preposterous," Mr Vaugham said. "But I pray that you believe me. You did not tell Mr Temple I called you?"

"No. And I do not think he heard me come downstairs." Florence's heart beat fast. She felt as if the bog lapped at her ankles. "Did he do this?"

A shiver racked Mr Vaugham's body. "He woke me from slumber. Said that our dam had failed and that our excavation area was about to be lost. When we got there, it was fine. As I looked for the problem, he struck me. I… I think he pushed me into the bog. I lost consciousness."

Florence clutched the curtains for support. Her head

spun, body swaying. She could not give way to dizziness now. "But that would mean—"

As Mr Vaugham raised his head to her, she saw her own horror reflected in his eyes. "Mr Temple tried to kill me."

"He must have removed the key from my cottage. I'm locked out," Vaugham continued. "I don't know what to do. I must get as far away from here as possible, but I feel so weak, so cold…"

Florence shut her eyes. Mr Vaugham did not need a rabbit. He needed a heroine. If only Rosemary were here!

Florence did her best to imitate Rosemary's practical courage. "Come to the back door. I'll let you in."

The kitchen fire slumbered overnight, packed full with peat before Margot retired. Florence stirred up the coals with the poker. "Get out of as many of your wet things as you can."

Mr Vaugham pulled off his jacket and vest. As Florence wrung the garments over the kitchen sink, he stretched shaking hands towards the fire. "I'm so cold."

"A pot of tea will warm you up." Florence set the kettle to boil over the fire. Turning, she stifled a gasp.

The light from the fire played over Vaugham's face. A patch she'd taken as shadow was an ugly wound seeping across his forehead.

This was no accident, no misunderstanding. Florence

swallowed, feeling her blood turn to ice within her veins. This was deliberate.

Mr Vaugham swayed, steadying himself against the kitchen wall.

Florence grabbed a chair from the kitchen table. "Sit." She grabbed a cloth from the linen drawer and filled a basin at the sink. Kneeling beside Mr Vaugham, she dabbed at the wound.

Mr Vaugham shuddered, slumping back in the chair. He was not unconscious, but she did not think he was entirely awake. The shock was catching up with him. Florence placed her shawl around him and continued to bathe the wound.

The blood washed away, revealing a much smaller wound than she had feared. It seemed to have congealed. She decided to leave it be rather than risk it bleeding anew.

The kettle began to hiss.

Florence snatched it from the fire before its noise could rouse anyone. She poured the hot water into the tea kettle, her mind racing ahead of her actions. Once Mr Vaugham was warm, what then? He could not remain at the Old House. But where could he go for help?

"Here." She wrapped his hands around the cup of tea. "Get this inside you."

"Although I'm more of a coffee person, on this occasion, I won't insist." Mr Vaugham managed a ghost of his usual smile.

Florence's stomach lurched. Was he even well enough to leave? "How are you feeling?"

"Like hell alive." Vaugham coughed. "I beg your pardon, Miss Skelton. I wasn't thinking."

Florence stared at him helplessly. She was not equipped for this kind of situation. What on earth was one to do?

Carmilla would have known what to do at once. She would have come up with a scheme to get Mr Vaugham to safety and inform the local police. "The boat. We can take the boat to Aylesport, inform the police—"

Mr Vaugham choked on his cup of tea. "No. Not the police."

Florence frowned. "But we must inform them. Mr Temple tried to kill you!"

"Mr Temple is a respected historian, known to everyone in this vicinity as a former curate." Mr Vaugham rasped. "I'm no one—not even an Englishman. All he has to say is that I provoked him and that's it. I lose everything. He gets the respect of his countrymen for defending himself against a thug. Worse—your reputation would be compromised."

"Hang reputations. This isn't right!" But even as she spoke, Florence knew that Vaugham was correct. Mr Temple had all the power. They had none. "What can we do?"

"I will take the boat," Mr Vaugham said. "I can get to the station, take the train away. I have friends in Cambridge. As long as I don't charge Mr Temple, he's got no reason to bother with me again."

Florence nodded slowly. "And me?"

Mr Vaugham set down his cup of tea. "Miss Skelton, what I am about to propose will test your courage. Mr Temple does not know that you know of his actions tonight. He has no reason to harm you."

"You suggest I stay behind, knowing what I know?" Florence's hand flew to her mouth, aghast. The idea was untenable.

"You should be quite safe as long as you are able to maintain your ordinary attitude towards him. You can then manufacture a reason to return to your family and leave as soon as you are able." Vaugham coughed. "Of course, if you wish to accompany me, I am prepared to marry you to preserve your reputation. However, I must warn you that being married to a foreigner brings its own set of challenges and hurdles."

"Quite apart from marrying for convenience." Florence sat on the stones before the fire. Mrs Vaugham's combative nature no longer alarmed her. She liked him, respected him, even. If she were to marry, she could do far worse.

Carmilla's rebuttal of the principal came to mind. Where there is no equality, there can be no respect—and without respect, no love. She thought, illogically, of Rosemary. If she ever married it would only be to someone who loved and valued her. "I shall remain. Write to me once you have an address. I will inform you of what is made of your disappearance here."

Mr Vaugham squeezed her hand. "I salute your courage, Miss Skelton. Not many women could do what you have done for me tonight." He made as if to stand. "I shall not delay—"

"Not in those clothes." Mr Vaugham's suit was mud stained. He would be remarked upon for sure. "I will fetch you something clean."

"Mr Temple took the key from my cottage. I've got no way to get inside."

Florence weighed their options. They could not risk Mr Temple realising that Mr Vaugham had survived. But neither could Mr Vaugham hope to reach his friends in Cambridge in his current state. He looked utterly disreputable. If he was stopped, word would reach Mr Temple of his survival...

Florence felt as if Rosemary stood at her elbow. There was only one thing to do. "I'm going to get the key from Mr Temple. If I fail, you'll need to run for the boat."

Mr Vaugham stared at her. "Miss Skelton, I—"

"Do not thank me yet." If she thought too hard about what she was about to do, she would lose the little nerve she possessed entirely. "Be ready for the worst."

Creeping up the stairs, Florence found it only too easy to imagine all the ways this could go wrong. Still, there was this consolation: if Mr Temple killed her and Mr Vaugham, her father could not lecture her on the impropriety of rescuing a bachelor of dubious antecedents.

She levered the door handle to Mr Temple's bedroom down. It did not creak. Florence held her breath, listening to the sounds within. Mr Temple's breath rasped as he lay abed. She peeked inside.

Two forms lay within. Mrs Temple shared her husband's bed. She lay still, so still that Florence could not even detect the rise and fall of her breathing. Mr Temple was another matter entirely. He muttered in his sleep.

Plagued by his guilty conscience? Florence's mouth twisted. He would not destroy Mr Vaugham, not if she could prevent it. She stepped forward, snatching up a suit jacket cast carelessly over a chair.

There was weight in one of the pockets that felt like a key. Florence backed out of the room. She examined her find in the hallway. Yes—this looked like the cottage key.

Mr Vaugham stood in the kitchen, clasping the poker. He relaxed as Florence entered. "You are braver than me, Miss Skelton. I could not help but imagine all that could go wrong."

"The less said about that, the better." He could not know her courage was only assumed. "Is this your key?"

"Indeed. You are a marvel." Mr Vaugham took it. "I'll leave it in the door. He can assume that I removed it."

Florence shook her head. "I must put it back. The longer he does not realise that you have survived, the better for your chances of reaching your friends."

Mr Vaugham squeezed her hand. "Words can never express my gratitude. Miss Skelton, you have saved my life."

Florence stood alone in the kitchen. A chill had settled over her. Mr Vaugham had the coldest hands of anyone she knew. She stepped closer to the fire, stretching out her hands. She must not think of what she had done, or what she risked should someone wake and discover her and Mr

Vaugham. Only if she pretended this was a story could she maintain her courage.

It seemed like hours before she heard the scuffle of boots on the steps outside. Mr Vaugham, now dressed in fresh clothes and with a hat covering the wound on his temple, pushed open the door. He held out the key. "Here."

Florence took it. "You're sure you'll find your way to Aylesport?"

He nodded. "I'll take the boat our now, but I will wait until dawn to row to Aylesport. If I leave the boat at the village I can walk down the railway tracks and catch the train at the next station."

"Be careful."

"Just what I was about to say." He hesitated. "Miss Skelton, if I can ever be of service to you, do not hesitate to call on me."

Florence glanced back to ascertain if the kitchen was still empty. It was. "My father is the vicar at Foxwood in Kent. He has been involved with mission work for many years, he may know your father. I do not think he will judge you unfairly. Tell him—tell him that I am in trouble. Send him to fetch me home."

Mr Vaugham nodded. "You can count on me, Miss Skelton." He stepped into the shadows. She heard his footsteps on the path.

Florence shut the door behind him. She stole up the stairs with Mr Temple's jacket in hand. Within minutes she had replaced it on the chair and was back in her bedroom, the door closed behind her.

Florence sank onto the floor beside her fire and closed her eyes. She was chilled to the bone, the purpose that had sustained her while Mr Vaugham was present deserting her entirely. Shivers racked her body, but though she was taut with fear, no tears came. How could she endure working for Mr Temple knowing he was prepared to murder?

23

Florence did not sleep at all. She made her way downstairs for breakfast, fear roiling in her stomach. This fear was different from last night, a slow dread that chilled her skin; made her thoughts slow and breathing hard.

If anyone asks I shall say I am unwell, she decided. It was not that far from the truth. Her head pulsed, a thudding pain. Her nerves were on edge, and her heartbeat rapid.

"Morning, Miss Skelton. May I pour you some tea?" Mr Temple beamed at her. "I have some bad news."

"Oh?" The expression she adopted whenever her father returned from the vestry meetings stood her in good stead.

"Mr Vaugham has had to leave us. He made his departure overnight. He had only enough time to dash off a quick note."

Florence almost choked on her tea. She had not expected Mr Temple to lie so boldly. Still, if years of sitting in on the Christian Ladies Association meetings had taught her anything, it was how to keep a straight face. "That is a shame. I understood he found his work here enjoyable."

"He did. No, it is not through any dissatisfaction that he has left us. I infer something of a personal nature occurred." Mr Temple buttered a second piece of toast for himself.

"Most inconvenient from my perspective. I cannot employ another assistant until the next quarter, which is quite a blow. It shall set me back no end."

Florence discovered that her hands clenched around her cutlery. She forced herself to relax. "I am sorry to hear that. If I may be of any assistance…"

"It is not work a lady could assist with. I shall endeavour to make do with Graham."

Florence sat down to the typewriter, so highly strung that she mistyped more words than she spelled correctly. Despite the evidence that Mr Vaugham had gotten away and that Mr Temple was no wiser to her involvement, she could not dispel the fear that had been growing since the previous night.

Florence took a deep breath and a fresh piece of paper. Until her father came to fetch her, all she had to do was be meek, unobjectionable and invisible—and she'd done that her entire life. With renewed determination, she typed.

Mrs Temple echoed Florence's disappointment at the news that Mr Vaugham had left them. She seemed lost in thought over lunch. As Florence rose from the table to fetch her coat, Mrs Temple stopped her. "I beg your pardon, Miss Skelton, but I am in the mood to walk alone today. You will not take offence?"

"No, not at all." Keeping up the pretence of normality was tiring. Florence retreated to her room, shutting the door behind her with relief.

She opened the windows, looking out over the bogs. It was a rare fine day with no mist, and the reflection of the blue sky delineated water channels from the grass. Or what looked like grass from her window. Florence knew better than to trust those appearances.

Mrs Temple emerged from the house, a shawl around her shoulders. She adjusted it, knotting it over one shoulder, just like she had in the photo of the Celtic woman. She stood a moment, looking out at the bog and then, with the air of one who knew where she was going, strode over the grass.

Abandoning the path? Mrs Temple had lived all her life in Old House. If anyone could walk the bogs safely, it was her. Even so, Florence watched her with an uneasy feeling.

Finally, she turned aside. She must find some way to occupy herself or she would go mad. Her nerves were still on a fever's edge, and she had no one to talk to, no one to confide in. The Lepidopterists? She could not navigate her way back to them through the bog, but if she could get a message to them…

Florence opened the drawer where she kept her letter writing supplies. She had not opened the drawer since that last fateful letter to Rosemary. The pages still rested on top.

Rosemary.

Florence lifted the pages. How small their quarrel seemed in the face of Rosemary's absence! She longed for nothing more than Rosemary's cool head and practical notions. She'd have a plan—one that didn't involve waiting for rescue. But what else could she do?

Florence sighed, making the pages of Rosemary's letter rustle. As they did, the word 'embalming' caught her eye. Florence lifted the page.

It was a postscript, scrawled on the back of the letter. Florence must have overlooked it.

P.S. I almost forgot to answer your question. Mr Temple did talk to Mr Leighton about embalming. He wanted to know what steps Mr Leighton took to preserve the Hand of Glory, where he procured his formaldehyde, and if he had undertaken any research into the preservation of larger specimens. He seemed rather well informed already, with Mr Leighton remarking that he could not tell Mr Temple anything he did not already know. What is behind this question, rabbit? I hope you are not wondering how best to preserve your mortal remains. It seems to me rather premature to contemplate your departure.

Mr Leighton could tell Mr Temple nothing he did not already know. Florence found herself sitting on her bed with no memory of how she got there. She turned the paper over, thinking hard. Mr Temple was an archaeologist. He did not need to preserve specimens of any sort. The bog already did a thorough job of that, if she understood Mr Temple's notes on the subject. Certainly, one would not embalm pottery or jewellery. Embalming was for living things. Or once living things.

Something banged downstairs. Florence leaped to her feet. She stood, hands pressed to her heart. It was only the downstairs door. She looked out the window and saw Mr Temple making his way to the boathouse, Graham trailing behind.

Mr Vaugham had taken the boat. Florence shrank back from the window. The discovery now was inevitable. Was this what she had been dreading all day?

Her mind returned to the senselessness of the attack on Mr Vaugham. He was an able assistant, and he'd even stopped arguing with Mr Temple—not that Mr Temple had seemed perturbed by their debates. And as Mr Temple himself said, he could not do without an assistant so close to the reassessment of his sponsorship grants... If only she were already home!

Thinking of Foxwood gave her courage. The soonest Mr Vaugham could reach the vicarage was that evening. Her father might arrive as soon as tomorrow evening. If so, she must be ready to depart. Her trunk had been removed to an attic. With both Mr and Mrs Temple out of the house, this was the ideal time to retrieve it unnoticed.

Florence scurried up the stairs. The attic was never locked, and she had no trouble locating her trunk. As she heaved it towards the door, her eyes fell on the label of the almost identical trunk behind it. *Mrs L Rutherford.*

Mrs Rutherford—the former secretary. Florence set

down her trunk with an intake of breath. Mr Temple had told Miss Brickwell that Mrs Rutherford had left. Why, then, was her trunk still in the attic?

Perhaps she'd borrowed the trunk from the Temples, Florence reasoned. The label alone meant nothing.

Her hand rested on the latch. It was wrong to pry. Hadn't her parents warned her that idle curiosity was fatal in a woman?

Florence opened the trunk.

Clothing was stuffed haphazardly. Florence picked up the rust coloured dress on the top, shaking it out. Too short to fit Mrs Temple, too slender for Margot. She set it down and got a second shock—the brown calico dress resting beneath it looked very familiar.

Florence held the dress out before her. Yes. She'd seen this one on its wearer.

The pond woman.

It cannot be the same dress, Florence reasoned. She turned it over, her mind fighting against rising panic. She noted the mud stains, unable to stop herself comparing them against the damage done to Mr Vaugham's suit the night before. If Mr Temple had pushed Mr Vaugham into the bog…

The room swayed around her. Florence shut her eyes, steadying herself against the wall. The sponsorship grants. The attack on Mr Vaugham. Mr Temple's claims that there was a Celtic queen buried in the bog. Mrs Rutherford's disappearance and now her belongings, hidden in the attic. Could Mr Temple have created his own Celtic find? No, surely that was impossible!

Florence heard distant voices. She bundled the dresses back into the trunk and set her trunk in front of it before scurrying back to her room.

There was a rap at her door. "May I have a moment, Miss Skelton?" asked Mr Temple.

Florence opened her door.

"Ah, you're here." Mr Temple frowned at her. "Have you seen my wife?"

"Mrs Temple went for a walk by herself," Florence squeaked. "I don't believe she has returned yet."

"That would explain it," Mr Temple said. "It's nothing urgent. I just wanted to let her know that Graham's memory is getting worse."

Florence felt like her lungs were trapped in a vice. "Oh?"

"He neglected to tie up the boat and it has drifted away. He claims someone has taken it, but I know better. We're as secure at Old House as if we were on an island. I've sent him to the village to borrow a replacement."

Florence forced a smile. Once he arrived at the village, Graham would find the boat. "That is a concern. I trust Mrs Temple will return soon."

Mr Temple had already turned away. Florence shut her door and leaned against it. Her heart raced, head pounded. She could not endure much more of this.

24

Florence received an unexpected reprieve. Mr Temple sat down at the dinner table that night in marked good humour.

"Graham tells me that the weather tomorrow should be as fine as it is today. I propose that we take advantage of it with a trip to Hartlea. I have a few supplies that I need for my work, and I'm sure that you can think of plenty of shopping with which to occupy yourself, my dear." He nodded to his wife.

"That is no trouble." Mrs Temple's smile had a scornful edge. She looked to Florence. "How will you amuse yourself, Miss Skelton?"

"I do not yet know." Florence's voice sounded shaky to her own ears. She mustered a smile. "I am not familiar with Hartlea, having only had the merest glimpse of it from the train window." Truthfully, she'd not even had that.

"I suggest you take in the art gallery," Mr Temple said. "Very suitable for two women together. I would not even consider the museum—a very provincial affair, lacking in every respect. No, you must not visit the museum."

Mr Vaugham had spoken of the Hartlea museum—as the

place that held the body of the woman discovered in the bog. Florence gulped. She had to see her.

Mr Temple regarded her oddly.

"I beg your pardon, Mr Temple. Did you speak?"

"I remarked that you must dress warmly. Even with so bright a forecast ahead of us, the weather here is very changeable."

Florence did not know whether to pray for sunshine or rain. As she lay in bed that night, she weighed her options. She knew the routine at Old House and could be confident of maintaining control of her reactions. Yet, every day wore her resolve down even further. She could not keep this up much longer.

A trip to Hartlea might be just what she needed. It might even afford her an opportunity to escape…

Escape—and let Mr Temple suspect his actions were known, putting Mr Vaugham at risk? Florence's heart sank. She must endure until her father fetched her away. The soonest he might arrive was tomorrow evening. Florence took a deep breath and steeled herself for sleep. She could endure one more day.

Her sleep was shallow. Florence woke with the impression she'd been lying not in her bed, but at the bottom of one of the water channels, looking up through its rippled surface at the grey sky, reeds bobbing in the wind. The morning sun, bright in the blue sky, seemed obscene in comparison.

Despite the circumstances, Florence found her spirits rising as she climbed out of the boat at Aylesport. Mr Temple was in holiday spirits, bustling here, there, and everywhere, buying tickets, getting his wife a blanket, Florence a bottle of lemonade.

Not for the first time Florence wondered if she had been misled. If Mr Vaugham had fallen, injured himself… Yet that did not explain why Mr Temple had lied about Mr Vaugham's departure.

It was a short train ride to Hartlea. Florence stood in the stone square before the station, soaking in the noise and bustle with renewed appreciation. She had not before realised how quiet Old House was, or how much she'd missed the community at Foxwood.

Mr Temple consulted his watch. "We made good time. I shall leave you to your errands. We will meet here to take the return train at four."

Mrs Temple inclined her head. "This way, Miss Skelton. You do not object to getting the household shopping out of the way first?"

Mrs Temple always asked what Florence wanted as an afterthought. Florence could not resent it. With her regal air, she couldn't imagine Mrs Temple not getting her own way.

As they walked down Hartlea's Main Street, Florence looked around for the museum. She soon spotted it, a severe grey stone building with Greek pillars that emphasised its scholarly intent.

Mrs Temple entered the tailors, and the familiar tradition began. Rolls of fabric were brought out, the merits of wool, calico, cotton, and silk debated, and the latest styles weighed against the considerations of wear and cost. Florence knew the arguments for and against wool as well as anyone, but she had difficulty applying herself to the question of navy or forest for Mrs Temple's new dress. Her thoughts returned to the museum.

It was ridiculous to suppose she would discover anything there. Even if what she feared was true, she did not know Mrs Rutherford to identify her remains. She would learn nothing.

Yet, as if pulled by clammy hands towards the building, Florence was drawn to the museum.

"You seem distracted, Miss Skelton. Looking at the museum?" Mrs Temple remarked. "As Ignatius says, it is most disappointing."

Florence inclined her head. "I do not mean to be preoccupied."

"It is only natural. This is your first time in Hartlea, after so long at Old House. Naturally, you long to take in as much of the town as you can. Choosing a dress is only interesting for she who is intending to wear it." Mrs Temple's smile was sardonic without being offensive.

Florence blushed. "I don't suppose I can be of service in any other way?"

Mrs Temple looked around the store, her eyes resting on a roll of crepe. "I shall need to look in at the milliners myself, but I do not see any reason you couldn't purchase my needle-work supplies. I have the thread here, so you know the colours I need more of."

Carrying the responsibility of running errands for Mrs Temple felt like the first time Florence had been allowed to carry the tea tray into the Ladies Fellowship meeting. She made her way down Main Street to the haberdashers and spent an agreeable twenty minutes finding the right threads and choosing needles. Florence made her way back down the street.

Instead of entering the tailors, Florence glanced through the windows. Mrs Temple and the assistant were now surrounded by rolls of crepe and taffeta, debating the relative merits of each. Florence strolled across the road, dropped tuppence into the collection box, and walked into the Hartlea museum.

She could not fault the Temple's description of the museum as 'inadequate.' The building has pretensions the dimly lit room did not live up to. The walls were lined with a series of display cabinets, more forming an island in the centre of the room. A taxidermy lion stood at one end of the room, and an immense tortoise shell hung from the ceiling. The curator, a dissipated looking young man, glanced up, surveyed Florence and returned to his newspaper.

Florence drifted around the room, but it was soon apparent that the bog lady was not there. She approached the curator. "Excuse me. I understood that your museum had in its collection a certain…" She paused. Her natural delicacy revolted at the thought of describing what she was there to see.

"You're after the body." The curator set down his paper and stood, taking a key from the wall. "We had to move it. There were objections it wasn't decent."

Florence blushed. What did that say about her interest? "I don't—"

"It is rather a shame to consign her to a back room. She is by far the most interesting item in our collection." The curator led the way to a door at the back. "But I don't know that I'd like to continue to share the main room with her, either. She's rather too well preserved. I keep expecting her to sit up and demand an explanation for this treatment."

Florence wished herself back at the tailor shop. "No one knows who she is?"

"That's not as surprising as it sounds. The bogs are treacherous, and over the years many local people have vanished in them. There's no shortage of women she could be. The problem is no one can identify her." The curator turned his key in the lock and pushed open the door. "Ladies first. Don't mind the smell. In the absence of the natural preservation afforded by the bog, we make use of embalming agents."

Florence stepped into a smaller room. She was at first surprised by the Greek pottery and a few statues on the shelves, but a closer look revealed an anatomical accuracy at odds with good taste. This room was the repository of anything that might offend.

Florence looked around for something safer on which to rest her eyes. In the centre of the room was a coffin with a glass lid. Her spirits sank. No turning back now.

"Not the most good looking of women," the curator continued. "But you wouldn't forget that face. Which, I suppose, only adds to the mystery."

Florence made a non-committal noise, gathering her courage. She walked up to the head of the coffin and looked down.

The woman lay as one sleeping, eyes closed, lips parted, black hair brushed off her face. A woven woollen blanket clothed her from the neck down. She looked as though she slept.

The curator was right, one would not forget that face. Florence knew it well. The lady who had pushed her into the pond in Foxwood village, and who she had seen walk into the bog, lay in the glass coffin.

25

Florence staggered through the door into the museum proper. Her legs gave way, and she folded onto the ground, skirts billowing out around her like an accordion.

"I should have mentioned the formaldehyde." The curator sidestepped around her. "It takes some people that way. I'm told it's very unpleasant." He thrust a chair at Florence. "No sense of smell, that's me."

Florence stared at him.

"Take your time." The curator looked at his watch. "You're not the first to come over faint after viewing the bog lady."

The horror of her discovery crashed over Florence a second time. The bog lady of Hartlea museum and the lady who had tried to kill her—had spoken to her, warned her—were the same. "How—how recently did she die?"

"No one knows." The curator resumed his chair. "But if you're asking how long she's been resident, well, it's longer than I've been curator, and I took this job three years ago."

Florence heaved herself to her feet, using the chair to steady herself. "You're not mistaken?"

"I'm hardly likely to forget, am I?" The curator glared at

his paper. "Four years of study to rusticate in this glorified storeroom!"

Florence put her hands over her face. The bog lady had been dead for over three years. Yet, she had appeared to Florence in Foxwood and walked into the bog in Aylesport... Both times she had shown no sign of needing to breathe. The only explanation was too horrible to contemplate.

Her hands were so cold...

Florence repressed a sob. Now was no time to go to pieces.

"You will be all right." The curator peered at her. "Usually all people need is a bit of fresh air."

"I'm sure you're right." Florence focused her attention on the wobble in her legs. When she was sure her limbs would obey her, she stood. So far, so good. "I'll just be on my way."

"No need to rush, Miss Skelton." A rustle of skirts. Mrs Temple stood by a diorama of a Roman outpost. "We have plenty of time."

Florence's legs turned to jelly. She sank back on the chair, an expression of unmitigated horror on her face. Discovered! Surely Mrs Temple must know why she'd come to the museum and what she'd seen…

"Mrs Temple!" The curator scrambled to his feet with an energy at odds with his previous lethargy. He bowed, almost colliding with a display case of arrowheads. "I don't suppose you remember me—Alistair Witt. I was an undergraduate student some years ago, and your husband allowed me to visit his excavations."

Mrs Temple's smile was indulgent. Demonstrations like this were nothing new to her. "Of course I remember you, Mr Witt. Ignatius remarked how knowledgeable you were about Roman weaponry."

Mr Witt turned a pleased shade of red. "Mr Temple is too generous. Is he keeping well?"

Florence's heart sank. Mr Witt was an admirer of Mr

Temple's. If she voiced her suspicions or asked for his help, he would think her hysterical or addled by the shock of viewing the Bog Lady.

"He is tolerably well," Mrs Temple remarked, standing beside Florence. "At this time of year, he has a lot on his mind."

"Grant season." Mr Witt nodded with an air of understanding. "The decision to abandon the draining of the Aylesport bog must be a great relief to him."

"Indeed," Mrs Temple said. "Although we would prefer that it did not happen in so tragic a manner."

Tragic? Florence stayed still. Although Mrs Temple faced Mr Witt, she was sure that the woman watched her.

"Quite, quite," Mr Witt murmured, tugging at his collar. "A very rum thing, three members of the Board all drowning like that... It does not seem like it can be coincidence."

"No," Mrs Temple agreed. "The board made a dangerous enemy when they set their sights on Aylesport." Her slender fingers rested on Florence's shoulder, ice-cold against her skin.

"I should not be surprised if that was the case," Witt continued. "Some local lunatic, no doubt. He might even be present in Hartlea now."

"Careful Mr Witt. You will alarm my friend. She might think you refer to yourself." Mrs Temple's manner was that of an arch society hostess.

Mr Witt glanced down at Florence as if surprised that she was still there. "Are you feeling any better?"

Mrs Temple's fingers tightened on her shoulder.

"Much," Florence said. "I must apologise for the bother I've caused. I don't know what came over me."

"Think nothing of it." Mr Witt bowed. "It is always a pleasure to see you, Mrs Temple."

"Too kind," Mrs Temple murmured. "We must be on our way. We have much to do in Hartlea."

Florence felt powerless to resist as Mrs Temple put her arm in hers, drawing her towards the door.

Take hold of yourself!

Her only chance was to act as though nothing was wrong. "Thank you again for your help, Mr Witt."

Once they were outside in the street, Mrs Temple spoke. "It was unwise of you to visit the museum, Miss Skelton—most unwise."

Florence's brain stalled. "I—"

"Did you find the thread I was looking for?"

It was an effort to return to the world of sewing thread and needles. "Yes. They had everything on your list."

"Splendid. In that case, we shall take lunch at the hotel." Mrs Temple continued down the street at a leisurely pace. "When Ignatius and I are in town, we always dine there. They have a restaurant separate from the public house, so I do not think it at all improper."

Florence's head throbbed with the effort of maintaining an ordinary appearance. "I am sure that if you approve it, the restaurant is quite satisfactory."

Mrs Temple's manner as she ordered luncheon for them both was as usual. "Ignatius has given me quite the list for the stationers. I suggest we go there first, and if we have any time remaining, take in the art gallery. You'll find it much more to your taste than the museum."

Florence flinched, missing her veal and scraping her knife against her plate. What did Mrs Temple mean by alluding to the museum? Could it be she did not know what Florence had discovered? "I hope so."

No—if what Florence feared was true, and the Bog Lady was indeed Mrs Rutherford, then Mrs Temple must know. Mrs Rutherford had lived under her roof for many months, and her body was perfectly preserved. Recognition must be inevitable—that is, assuming Mrs Temple had seen the exhibit.

Could she assume that? Florence smiled, shaking her head as Mrs Temple offered her a second cup of tea. She had not stepped inside the back room—but neither had she evinced any curiosity about its contents. "No, thank you. I am not used to so rich a luncheon. I shall struggle to finish my meal as it is."

Mrs Temple nodded. "Perhaps I have been extravagant. We rarely get the chance to treat ourselves, living in such seclusion as we do."

Seclusion? Florence chewed her veal, prolonging each mouthful as she thought. When the bog body was discovered, there must have been considerable local interest in its identification. Yet no one had recognised Mrs Rutherford. Not surprising if the Temples kept to the same solitary existence—

Florence choked. Mr Temple's forbidding of her to visit the village and his anger at learning Mr Vaugham had collected Florence from the station suddenly gained sinister implications. Was he trying to ensure Aylesport's inhabitants would be unable to identify Florence or Vaugham should they die under suspicious circumstances?

Mrs Temple glanced up from her cup of tea. "There is no rush, Miss Skelton. We have plenty of time to complete our errands."

"A sore throat, that is all. I've changed my mind—I would like a cup of tea." Florence gave her most enduring smile—the one that sustained her through the three hourly mothers and wives committee meetings.

After lunch, Florence walked with Mrs Temple to the stationers. She watched as Mrs Temple made the selections of inks and paper, giving her opinion on the choice of typewriter ribbon and other necessities. Mostly, she observed Mrs Temple herself.

Mrs Temple weighed her choice of notebooks, consulting the list given to her by Mr Temple with every evidence of wifely solicitude. It was more impossible than ever to guess what she thought. Had she connected the bog lady with Mrs Rutherford? What did she make of Florence's visit to the museum?

"This cannot be very interesting for you, Miss Skelton. Would you care to walk ahead to the gallery?"

Florence started. She was being given her freedom? "I don't wish to be a bother."

"It is no bother at all, and there are some landscapes that are worth seeing." Mrs Temple shooed her towards the door. "I will find you there."

In the art gallery, Florence stood in front of the one painting for over half an hour, but she could not have described it. What was Mrs Temple playing at? If she had guessed what Florence knew, why would she allow her the chance to escape?

Or was this a test? Florence wiped clammy hands on her skirts. If she attempted to flee, it would confirm to the Temples that Florence had uncovered their plot.

Calm. Florence steadied her breathing. She did not know whether Mrs Temple had conspired with her husband to kill Mrs Rutherford and present her to the world in the guise of a Celtic queen. But even if that dreadful suspicion was true, Mrs Temple could not know that that Mrs Rutherford had attempted to drown Florence—or that Florence had seen Mrs Rutherford since. She had no reason to think anything but ghoulish curiosity had taken Florence to the museum.

Besides, Mrs Temple had sent Mr Vaugham to the station to meet Florence. If she was cognisant of her husband's murderous schemes, surely she would not have done so.

Florence felt more herself with this realisation. When Mrs Temple joined her at the gallery, she managed to smile naturally.

The journey back to Old House was an ordeal. Florence

struggled to keep her revulsion towards Mr Temple in check. Her cheeks ached, her smile becoming fixed.

Mr Temple peered at her as he helped her ashore at the little pier. "Are you well, Miss Skelton? You do not seem in your usual spirits."

"I am a trifle tired," Florence admitted. "My nerves are on edge." She took a deep breath. "I am afraid I ignored your advice and looked in the museum. I found it upsetting—I was not at all prepared for what I saw."

She felt Mr Temple's hand go rigid. "You went to the museum?"

Mrs Temple put her hands on Florence's shoulders. "She's had a severe shock but has been doing her best not to let it distress us. An early night and she should be as right as rain in the morning."

"Yes—of course." Mr Temple released her hand. "I leave you in Ana's capable hands."

Mrs Temple saw Florence to her bedroom and had a light supper sent up to her. "The best cure for nerves is rest." She drew Florence's curtains. "Even if you cannot sleep, lying still should be of benefit."

Florence sipped the broth. "I'm sure you're right." Mrs Temple's desire to help her seemed earnest... But whether she was genuine or not, Florence had reached a decision. She had to leave the Temple's house at once.

As she lay still in bed, waiting until the other residents of Old House slept, Florence reviewed her plans. Mr Vaugham might navigate the bog by boat at night. She, however, could not. Her only hope was to search for the path that Miss Brickwell had taken to Old House and make her way to the lepidopterists's cottage.

It was a huge risk... But the thought of staying at Old House even one more day was unbearable. Florence pressed her lips together. It was not bravery that compelled her to take so great a risk, but fear. How much of a coward did that make her?

At last, the house was still and dark. Florence dressed without a candle, stealing downstairs in the dark. She took her cloak and a lantern from the kitchen and slipped outside.

The bleak landscape was even more impenetrable at night. Florence followed the path, retracing the steps she'd taken with Miss Brickwell. If only she hadn't been so tired! Was it here the path divulged—or there?

Florence caught herself on the brink of stepping into nothingness. She had reached Mr Temple's archaeological trench. Another step and she would have plunged into the pit. Florence took a deep breath—she'd come too far. She must retrace her steps.

Light glinted within the trench, the lantern reflecting on something metallic. Florence raised the lamp higher.

The light glinted on the brass buttons of a waistcoat. Above the shirt collar, she saw a familiar face, eyes closed as if in sleep. Only the gash at his temple revealed this was no ordinary slumber.

The lantern fell from Florence's nerveless fingers. She sank to her knees, muffling her scream with both hands.

It was Mr Vaugham.

26

Rippling water caught Florence's attention. She stirred, finding herself lying on a cold, harsh surface. Gravel stuck to her cheek as she sat, blinking at the dew-swept grass surrounding her.

Where...?

Mist hung in the surrounding air, the sky a dim grey. Morning had come without her realising it.

Florence staggered to her feet. She must have fainted. Her lantern had burnt itself out. She looked at the empty trench with a shudder, having no desire to reacquaint herself with its ghastly contents.

Poor Mr Vaugham! All this time, she'd imagined him with his friends. Instead, he'd never left Old House...

Another splash, closer now. A boat. Searching for her? Florence cast around for a hiding place. The bog was bare of bushes, trees, or rocks. There was nothing to hide herself behind, and she could not rely on the mist.

A patch of reeds bobbing in the slight breeze caught her eye. Florence gathered her skirts and, forcing herself not to hurry, waded into the bog. The water was as cold as if it were still the height of winter. She crouched within the rushes, hardly daring to breathe.

Just in time.

The boat pulled up to the shore, Mr Temple at the oars. He waded ashore, drawing the boat onto the grass. He turned, approaching the trench.

The lantern! Florence swallowed. She'd left it where it was.

Mr Temple saw it just as she did. He picked it up, turning it over in his hands. "Warm." He glanced around.

Florence shut her eyes, unable to suppress a tremor. She could not take this tension.

She heard a clink as he set the lantern down, followed by a thud. Mr Temple grunted. By the sounds of things, he was exerting himself.

Florence risked a peek. Mr Temple heaved Mr Vaugham's body out of the trench and dragged it towards the boat. She closed her eyes, hot tears stinging her cheeks.

Another splash as Mr Temple pushed the boat back into the water, and then the regular ripple of oars. Florence stayed unmoving, listening as the boat pulled away. Florence readied herself. As soon as Mr Temple was out of earshot, she could take off across the bog in search of the lepidopterists.

Although she could no longer see Mr Temple, she could hear the splashing of the oars. And if she could hear him, he could hear her. Florence wrapped her arms around herself.

The chill bite had faded from the water, but her limbs felt numb. Her teeth chattered.

Finally, all was silent. Now was her chance. Florence gathered her strength, but her limbs did not obey her.

A large splash followed, large enough to send ripples to Florence's hiding place. She flinched as the water hit skin not yet inured to the cold. Before the water had resettled, she heard the scrape of oars against the surface of the bog. Mr Temple had returned.

This time he scanned the surrounding landscape. He knew someone had seen Mr Vaugham and now sought them amongst the bog.

Florence stayed motionless. Being discovered now would be fatal.

She heard the soft squelching of Mr Temple's boots on the path as he traversed the grounds of Old House. Every time she dared think him out of earshot, another noise would disabuse her of that notion.

At length, she heard a second steady tread. The whisper of skirts indicated that Mrs Temple had joined her husband.

"You're up early, my dear." What right had Mr Temple to sound so jovial? "To what do I owe this unexpected pleasure?"

"Miss Skelton did not come down for breakfast." Mrs Temple replied. "And she is not in her room."

"Oh?" Florence imagined Mr Temple's gaze resting on the lantern, his earlier suspicions confirmed. "It would appear that she, too, has left us."

"This has to stop," Mrs Temple said.

Mr Temple's reply was icy. "I am your husband. It is not your place to order me—or question me. I know what I am about."

There was a moment's pause before Mrs Temple replied. "These waters are sacred. You defile them with your actions."

"These bogs were a place of ancient sacrifice, to be consigned to them an honour accorded only to the greatest of leaders and their most trusted servants. I seek only to raise them to their proper importance in the public eye."

There was a slight pause before Mrs Temple replied. "Has it ever occurred to you that those who sleep here may wish to remain unknown?"

"I am in no mood for female nonsense," Mr Temple

snapped. "I will have my discovery, even if I have to produce it myself. Miss Skelton's absence has quite upset my plans. Send Graham and Margot to look for her. We cannot allow her to reach the town."

Mrs Temple glided away, but her words drifted behind her. "You disturb these waters at your own peril."

Mr Temple stood for a long moment. "If only she were not so well known. She would have made a splendid queen."

A few minutes later, Margot and Graham joined Mr Temple.

"Miss Skelton has gone for an early morning walk. We fear she has become lost in the bog," Mr Temple told them. "She cannot have gotten far. She does not know the bog like we do. Find her and bring her home." He paused. "It's possible that she may tell you some wild tale. She is hysterical and being lost in the bogs may disturb her. Ignore any such tales and bring her back here, forcefully, if necessary."

Florence, peering out through the reeds, saw nothing but passive acceptance on Graham and Margot's stony faces. She could have wept. There would be no mercy there.

Graham and Margot soon disappeared into the mist, leaving only their footsteps behind them. Mr Temple returned to the house.

Florence stared at the boat. Dare she take it? She did not know how to row... But this might be her only chance of escape. She stood—only to catch the sound of the house door closing. Florence sank back into the reeds.

Mr Temple strode back down the path, making for the boat. He wore a smart suit, rowing in the direction of town.

Florence watched him go. She was safe for the moment in the reeds. She was cold through and through, but she did not seem to be in any danger of detection. Mr Temple was no doubt going to discover if anyone had seen her in the village. Once he learned she had not left the bog, he would return to continue his search. If Florence could steal the boat on his return, she still had a chance.

❧

Remaining in her hiding place became more of a problem. Florence's legs ached with cramp and cold. She longed to stretch them. Every time she thought she might risk it, a sudden sound had her shrinking back into the reeds.

It was hopeless. She had no chance of escape. All she did was prolong her misery. Better to give herself up now, or just let herself sink into the bog and oblivion...

No. Florence took firm hold of her thoughts. She could not give up. Rosemary—Rosemary would despise her.

Rosemary. Even numbed with cold and fear, the image of Rosemary standing before Mr Skelton brought a rush of blood into Florence's cheeks. Rosemary had thought her brave. She was mistaken, but Florence could pretend—

Pretend, that was it! The circumstances would not daunt Carmilla, grim as they were. She would take action. Florence massaged her numb limbs, moving them as much as she dared. What would Carmilla do in this situation?

Imagining a new adventure for Carmilla helped take Florence's mind off her ordeal. So much so, it seemed no time at all before she heard the dip of oars and felt the ripples presaging Mr Temple's return.

Florence went still. This was her chance. She would seize the boat as soon as Mr Temple was far enough away.

"It is a very lucky coincidence that I ran into you, Horace. You see the difficulties you would have had in finding the place—or that Miss Skelton must have had leaving it."

Was that...? No, it couldn't be!

"Yes. I am astonished Florence attempted it at all." It was —her father's voice, a grim note in it.

Florence almost gave her hiding place away in her shock.

Her father, here! So Mr Vaugham had warned him after all—but no, Mr Vaugham had not left Old House. What had brought Mr Skelton to Aylesport?

"I hope you're able to shed some light on this occurrence," Mr Temple said. "I do not know Miss Skelton as well as you, but it strikes me as unusual behaviour for so thoughtful a young woman."

The scrape of the boat on the grass obscured Mr Skelton's reply. Florence heard the two men walk towards the house. Should she hail her father? No—alerting Mr Skelton to her presence might put him in danger. Mr Temple had killed twice already that she knew of. She could not risk her father becoming his third victim.

Nor could she leave him alone with Mr Temple. Florence looked at the boat. She must endure a bit longer.

It did not seem much longer at all before the men returned, the angry crunch of Mr Skelton's footsteps indicating he was in a temper. "I can only apologise again for the inconvenience my daughter has caused you, Mr Temple. I had no idea that she was even contemplating this."

"Nor had I. The letter she left behind was shock enough, although it gave no hint of her plans," Mr Temple said.

Letter? Florence pressed a hand over her mouth in shock. She'd almost forgotten the handwriting game and the letter she had written at Mr Temple's dictation. It had seemed innocent at the time. Had she penned her own demise?

"The letter from the publishing house provides ample indication of her intentions. She has made for London, seduced by the prospect of fame and adulation." Mr Skelton's sternness made Florence, chilled as she was, tremble anew. "I wash my hands of her."

"You must not be too harsh on her," Mr Temple said, helping Mr Skelton into the boat. "It seems she was encouraged in her reckless undertaking."

"Yes. I shall have a lot to say to Miss Scott for her part in my daughter's undoing." Mr Skelton sat rigidly in the boat. His face was set with anger. Florence, though she tried her best to find it, could discern any sign of grief or even sorrow. Was he so easily reconciled to her loss?

Florence slumped forward, her eyes blurring. She was unprepared for the keen pain of this abandonment.

~

Some time later, Florence realised she could hear the boat returning. Mr Temple returning from taking her father to the village, no doubt. This was it: her last chance for escape.

What was the use? Where could she go? Not Foxwood, not knowing how little her father cared for her—nor could she endure his anger again. She had no other friends—

Rosemary?

Florence caught her breath. Rosemary would be shocked at her cowardice, but she would not cast her aside. No, Rosemary would not endure a man like Temple escaping unpunished. Rosemary would know what to do.

Florence readied herself for action.

Mr Temple pulled the boat ashore. He marched off, evidently with a destination in mind.

Now! Florence heaved herself to her feet.

After hours in the cold water, her body was sluggish and unresponsive. Florence took only one step before her legs gave way. She fell onto her knees with a splash that echoed through the swamp like a gunshot.

No time to hesitate. Florence muffled her sob, forcing herself forward on her hands and knees. She used the reeds to pull herself onto the shore. Her long skirts threatened to pull her down into the bog, heavy with water. It was all Florence could do to shove the boat into the water and fall headfirst into it.

The boat tipped as she struggled to right herself. Suddenly, it went still.

Mr Temple held the boat, a thin smile tugging at his lips. "Excellent! You have saved both of us a lot of trouble. I congratulate you on your good sense, Miss Skelton."

Florence could not remember ever being so cold. She waded through the bog. Her skirts dragged her backwards, making each step an effort. Her hair had come loose, straggling down her neck in thick tendrils. At least she'd stopped trembling. Now she need not worry her chattering teeth would give her away.

Florence halted, water swirling around her. Where was she going? She had to get out of the bog; she knew that much. She had to escape Mr Temple...

Her head ached. Florence put a hand to her brow. Mr Temple had found her. And then...?

She must have escaped. Otherwise, why would she be here? Florence looked around.

She stood knee-deep in water, surrounded by the unrelenting sameness of the bog. The mist had lifted, but in its place was the deepening twilight. Soon she would not see at all.

Florence contemplated this difficulty without fear. The urgency of her situation no longer worried her. A strange peace had settled over her.

Exhaustion, no doubt. One could only take so much fear. Florence weighed her options.

In the distance, a light caught her eye. A will-o'-the-wisp, no doubt. But even a marsh candle was better than no candle, and she might be able to warm herself by its flame. Florence turned her steps towards it.

She made slow progress through the bog, heavy skirts and numb limbs weighing her down. It was some time before she realised the will-o'-the-wisp was no illusion, but a lantern, and it was even longer still before she realised that the cloaked figure holding it aloft as she stood, waiting on the shore of Old House, was Mrs Temple.

Florence kept walking. Her capacity for thought or even for shock was entirely depleted.

Mrs Temple did not seem surprised by Florence's disorderly appearance. She waited until Florence had drawn even with her before speaking. "You will be cold. Come with me."

Florence bowed her head and followed.

Mrs Temple walked towards the stone dairy adjoining Mr Vaugham's cottage. Florence had not been inside either building before. The dairy had wide wooden doors for the animals and a narrower door to one side. Mrs Temple opened the narrow door.

Graham sat within, crouching by the fire. He looked up as his mistress entered. As his eyes lighted on Florence, his expression did not show even the slightest surprise.

"This way." A narrow stairway led to the second floor, disclosing a very bare bedroom. Evidently, this was where Graham slept.

Mrs Temple opened a cupboard. "Through there."

Was she about to be locked in a cupboard? But as Florence knelt, she discovered there was a room on the other side. This must be the second floor of Mr Vaugham's cottage.

Inside was a fireplace with a lit fire. Florence crawled towards it, holding out her hands to the flame.

"You will stay out of sight here," Mrs Temple had followed her through the cupboard passage. "Ignatius must not see you."

Florence glanced up at her, remembering the conversation she'd overheard. Mrs Temple knew of her husband's actions, but was not in league with him? "What do you intend—" She gasped.

A figure sat in a chair in the far corner of the room. She did not stir, but Florence recognised her at once. The pond woman—Mrs Rutherford.

Mrs Temple followed her gaze. "You need not worry about Mrs Rutherford. She was sent to warn you, no more. It is a pity that you did not heed my warning."

Mrs Rutherford raised her head. She looked at Florence with the same disinterest she'd seen reflected in Graham's eyes.

"A warning? But she tried to drown me!" Florence's hand went to her throat.

"She meant only to scare you away." Mrs Temple stooped, throwing some more peat onto the flames.

Mrs Rutherford did not seem to harbour any strong feelings towards Florence now. She didn't even stir.

Florence crept closer to the fire. It felt wrong to turn her back on the other woman, but she wanted the fire's warmth so much. *I am your future.* She swallowed, tasting copper in her throat as she remembered Mrs Rutherford's words. *Should you leave Foxwood, this is what awaits.*

But Mrs Rutherford was dead, her body lying in the Hartlea museum. "How is this possible?"

"This is a sacred place of old," Mrs Temple said. Her voice had a melodic note that gave her words, simple as they were, a strange beauty. "There is power in these waters. The ancient people of this land knew it. They laid their queen in these waters, so she might forever guard them. With her they placed a loyal manservant and her most trusted attendants.

The four of them protected the bog, the treasures of their people, and their resting place. They remain here to this day, guarding the bog against those who would destroy it."

This was no fairy tale. Florence gazed into Mrs Temple's beautiful, distant face, saw again the photograph of her dressed in the fashion of a long distant time. Impossible! her mind protested. But looking at Mrs Temple, Florence knew it to be true.

"But Mr Temple—"

"A gamble," Mrs Temple said. "The bog was in danger of being destroyed. A new method of extracting peat by mechanisation would have destroyed everything we hold dear. The owners did not care for the wishes of the villagers. The new curate spoke of the interest of the bog from an archaeological perspective. I provided him with a few treasures. The interest they raised allowed us to preserve the bog—and raised Mr Temple's ambitions. He was not content."

Florence shuddered. So this implacable woman had married him. All to preserve the bog, as she had been doing for untold centuries.

"Wring out your clothing," Mrs Temple instructed. "It will dry faster that way. I will send for you if I have need of you. Otherwise, remain here out of sight." She made her way back through the cupboard. The click of a lock followed.

Florence looked at Mrs Rutherford. She sat in the chair still, her eyes closed. To all appearances, she was asleep.

Florence hesitated, but the puddle of water forming around her decided things. Her cold fingers fumbled with the many buttons, but finally she peeled her dress off. She wrung out her dress into the ash bucket and spread it out over the floor to dry. Then, she wrung out her petticoats.

Mrs Rutherford did not stir.

Florence studied her. Here was the proof of Mrs Temple's story. She had seen Mrs Rutherford's corpse, seen her move, heard her talk. And yet, despite the many proofs, her mind still refused to accept this as real.

Florence crouched beside the fire. She needed to get warm, shake off the chill that still hung over her and made her thoughts and body sluggish. Yes—once she was warm, she would be able to make sense of this.

Steam rose off her petticoats. Gradually, they dried. Florence picked out her hairpins and used her fingers to comb her hair into order. The familiar action gave her a sense of purpose. Yes, she might face an inexplicable situation of strange and unknown horror, but she still had standards. She was a vicar's daughter.

The bite of her emotions was all the more painful for being unexpected. Florence's fingers stalled, the pin slipping to the floor. She was no longer a vicar's daughter. "Father…"

The fire crackled and shifted, a hunk of peat sliding from the grate. Florence grabbed it and flung it back into the flames before it could catch. She shook her hand, looking about for something to use as a bandage. It was only then she realised her fingers didn't hurt.

Florence held her hand out, examining it closely. Smudges of ash showed where she had grasped the peat, but there was no reddened skin, nothing that indicated a burn. Her flesh felt just as cold as when she'd first climbed out of the bog.

"No."

Florence grasped her wrist, feeling for a pulse.

None.

She hadn't escaped the bog. She was part of it.

"What have you done with Miss Skelton?"

The voice was familiar, and yet entirely wrong. What would Rosemary be doing in Aylesport?

Florence smiled. She still sat beside the fire. Out of habit, she'd dressed herself—she could only imagine her mother's horror if she had died wearing nothing but her undergarments. Some of the cold had eased, but a weight too heavy for her to bear alone still oppressed her.

She had done everything right. Obeyed all the rules—or done her best to obey them. She was a nice, well brought up girl. How could she be dead?

"I beg your pardon, Miss Scott. If you seek Miss Skelton, you must seek her elsewhere." Mr Temple sounded annoyed. "She has left—as her father no doubt informed you."

She might hallucinate Rosemary's voice, but Mr Temple? Never. Florence climbed to her feet. The rest and the fire had been good for her. She moved more easily. Peeking out the window, she saw Mr Temple standing below, dressed for excavating. Facing him, her hands on her hips, her chin lifted and her eyes blazing, ready for battle was—

"Rosemary!" Florence blinked, but the vision did not depart. She did not imagine this. Rosemary was there!

Rosemary was in great peril. Florence gulped, looking for the latch to open the window. There might still be time to warn her—

The window did not open outwards. Florence looked back to the scene before her with growing alarm.

"I know what you told Mr Skelton," Rosemary said. "And I do not buy it. I know for a fact that Miss Skelton has not gone to London in search of a career as an author. I want to find her."

"She was here recently," a third voice added. Julian shuffled his feet behind Rosemary. "She's still close."

Had Rosemary and Julian come all the way from Foxwood to find her? Florence blinked. Her family might have written her off, but her friends had not…

Mr Temple gestured for them to follow him with ill grace. "I'm a busy man. I'm already behind schedule as it is, having to replace both my assistant and my secretary. I've no time to entertain wayward children. Come and see Miss Skelton's room for yourself. I assure you, I am not hiding her."

Florence thumped on the window glass. If she wanted to preserve her friends, she needed to do something. She could not let Rosemary and Julian fall victim to Mr Temple. "Run! Don't go inside—he's dangerous!"

Julian glanced up, a puzzled expression on his face, but Rosemary had already stepped inside Old House. He followed a moment later.

"No!" Florence stared after them. Mr Temple had not hesitated to kill her. He would not show Rosemary and Julian any mercy, either. She had failed them—just as she had failed everyone else. She'd disappointed her parents, left her sister Hannah alone. Not only had she proven herself unworthy of Rosemary's regard, but in her cowardice she'd summoned Rosemary to her death. She'd even endangered Julian, who was nothing to do with the situation at all.

Florence sagged against the windowpane, the glass cool against her cheek. Was this all that awaited her, an eternity of disappointment and despair? She deserved nothing more. She was only courageous in her stories…

Florence caught her breath. Imagining Carmilla's bravery had given her strength before. She could use that again now.

Mrs Rutherford opened her eyes as Florence rattled the cupboard door. "It's locked. There's no way out until we're let out."

"I'm not waiting here while he murders my friends." Florence eyed the small attic room. The only ways out were the windows. She picked up the metal tongs beside the fire and smashed them into the glass.

Mrs Rutherford shook herself, standing. "You can't do that."

"I just did." Using the butt of the poker, Florence knocked the remaining glass out of the windowpane. She dropped the poker out the window and seized the frame. It would be a tight squeeze, but she could just wriggle through.

Bother her skirts! Florence squirmed, dangling out the window.

"You'll fall," Mrs Rutherford warned. "You'll never survive."

Florence stared at the drop before her. It was not the sort of fall people walked away from… But she was already dead. "I have nothing to lose." Florence heaved herself into nothingness.

She had just a moment to feel alarm before she hit the ground. Was the crunch the impact of hitting ground, or was it her bones breaking?

The fall had not killed her, but she had not escaped unscathed. One arm did not obey her, but with the other she could roll onto her back. Mrs Rutherford peered from the cottage window as Florence took an inventory of herself. One arm and one leg didn't move. Broken, no doubt—but Florence did not feel pain.

She lay still. The fall had not hurt her, but she was far from unscathed. Her thoughts drifted in and out of darkness. When Florence stirred next, the sunlight had dimmed.

Evening! Florence rolled onto her knees. She had no time to lose. Anything might have happened to Rosemary and Julian by now—

All her limbs moved at her direction. Florence wobbled to her feet and found that one leg was less steady than the other, but she could stand.

She'd healed? Florence shook her head. She could wonder about that later. Right now: Rosemary.

A rattle called her attention to the window above. Mrs Rutherford leaned out. "Let me out," she hissed. "I would have my revenge."

Florence weighed her options. Mrs Rutherford had tried to kill her twice… But they'd been alone together in the attic for hours, and the other woman had not once tried to harm her. "There is a young woman and a boy here. They know nothing of the Temple's plans. You will leave them alone."

Mrs Rutherford nodded, a gleam in her eyes. "I care nothing for them. Give me Mr Temple. That's all I want."

Florence took a step back, appalled at the menace in the other woman's voice. She looked around. Old House looked deserted, but she knew that Graham and Margot would be nearby, to say nothing of the Temples. She was in no position to be choosy about her allies. "All right."

Florence crept through the dairy, back up the staircase to the bedroom. The key to the cupboard passage was still in the lock. She turned it, and Mrs Rutherford pushed the door open at once. "If you only knew how long I have been waiting for this moment!"

Florence shuddered. "Remember, no harm is to come to my friends."

Mrs Rutherford did not appear to hear her. She made her way down the stairs, pausing only to pick up a poker from the fireplace.

Florence followed her into Old House. Mrs Rutherford knew where she was headed. She didn't glance around her as she entered the kitchen, making straight for the study.

Mr Temple sat at his desk with a candle beside him. He looked up from his papers with a scowl. "I told you, I do not wish to be disturbed—" His face blanched, eyes bulging as he saw Mrs Rutherford in the doorway. "You!"

Mrs Rutherford smiled, stepping into the study. "Me."

Florence followed, casting a quick look around the room. No sign of Rosemary or Julian here. Where were they?

Mr Temple made to rise, but his legs gave way. He propelled himself backwards on the floor, his gaze travelling from Mrs Rutherford to Florence. "You're a figment of my imagination. You're not real."

Mrs Rutherford advanced towards him. She hefted the poker. "You must answer for your treatment of me." She brought the poker down.

Mr Temple rolled out of the way, barely escaping the blow. He darted across the study, seizing the bell pull. "Help —Graham, help! There is a madwoman—"

Mrs Rutherford swung the poker again. This time, the blow connected. Mr Temple collided with his desk, sending papers and candle to the floor. He cried out, turning to face his attacker. "Please—have mercy, I beg you!"

"You showed me no mercy." Mrs Rutherford's eyes glinted with more animation than Florence had seen her display yet. "So I have none for you." She brought the poker down. When she raised it again, it was stained in blood.

Florence shuddered, shielding her eyes with her hands. She could not block out Mr Temple's groans, nor the dull thump of the poker striking again and again, nor the crackle of the fire—

Fire? Florence's eyes flew open.

The toppled candle had caught on the spilled papers, and the blaze had reached the carpet. "Stop! The fire will spread!"

The door flung open. Graham stood in the doorway, face impassive as he surveyed the scene.

Mr Temple spat blood onto the floor. "Graham, subdue this woman. She is—"

Mrs Rutherford caught him another blow. She raised the poker to continue her bloody work. Graham grabbed for it, attempting to wrestle it from her.

Florence ran to the fire. She stomped on the rug, but it was too late—the flames had caught the desk. As she watched, they jumped to the curtain.

It was hopeless. She could not stop the fire. She had only one option: to find Rosemary and Julian before the house was ablaze proper.

29

Florence ran for the stairs. "Rosemary! Julian!" Mr Temple had offered to show them her room. Florence flung the door open, but the room was empty.

She ran down the hallway, throwing open every door she could find. "Rosemary! Julian!"

"Florence? We're in here!" A series of thumps came from the attic door.

Florence tried the handle, but though it turned, the door wouldn't open. "I can't open the door."

"We took the liberty of barricading ourselves in, Miss Skelton." Julian's thin voice piped up from the other side. "I don't wish to speak ill of your employer, but Mr Temple strikes me as being of a rather volatile nature."

"He tried to kill us!" Rosemary added.

Florence shut her eyes, struck by a dizzying fear. "Did he hurt you?"

"Not likely." Rosemary's tone was pure self-confidence. "Of course, we now have the problem of how to get out of here."

A heavy thump from the study rattled the house. "You need to get out right now. The house is on fire!"

"If it's not one thing…" Something heavy scraped along the attic floor. "Rabbit, you're all right?"

Florence went still. She put a hand to the wall to steady herself.

"Rabbit? Are you still there?"

"I'm here." She'd been preoccupied with rescuing Rosemary and Julian. She'd not thought that would entail revealing herself.

If Rosemary was furious with her before, that was nothing to how disgusted she must be learning Florence's fate. The revulsion and horror on Mr Temple's face rose before her. To have Rosemary look at her with such naked disgust? No—it was unbearable.

Florence took a shuddering breath and choked on smoke. She looked down. A red glow flickered in the downstairs passage. The fire had reached the hall. They were out of time.

"You must hurry!"

"This press is jammed. We're stuck!"

Florence tried pushing the door open. She soon saw the problem—Rosemary and Julian had toppled an old press but lacked the strength to now move it out of the way. "I'll push from this end." The three of their combined efforts moved the press just enough to make a large enough gap to squeeze through.

"You go first." Rosemary placed a hand on Julian's shoulder. "Go down the stairs and out the hall. Don't wait for us."

Julian wriggled through. "Father would say that's not very gentlemanly."

"It's not gentlemanly to argue with a lady." Rosemary gave him a shove. "Get out of here."

Florence tugged Julian the rest of the way through. "We'll follow as soon as we can."

Julian paused at the top of the stairs. "But—"

"Go!" Rosemary squeezed through the hole. "Someone needs to look for help."

That decided Julian. He squared his jaw and dashed down the stairs.

Dear God, please keep him safe. Florence took hold of Rosemary's hands and tugged.

"Why on earth do women have to have such hips?" Rosemary wriggled. "Goodness, your hands are cold."

Florence swallowed. No time for fear. "Keep it up." She pulled. She no longer had to worry about aching muscles or tired joints. With another tug, Rosemary slid free of the door.

"Thank you." Rosemary grasped Florence's hand, pulling herself to her feet. She limped but seemed otherwise unhurt. "I'll be fine. Let's get out of here."

As they hurried down the stairs, an unearthly howl split the air. Florence stopped still. "What is that?" It sounded like a wild creature, but she'd seen no animals capable of making that sound on the bog.

"Don't mind it now." Rosemary tugged her arm, hobbling towards the door. "This smoke will be a problem." Her eyes watered, and she held a hand over her mouth.

Of course, the smoke must be making it hard for her to breathe. Aside from an unpleasant smoky taste in her throat, Florence had no such problems. She pressed her handkerchief into Rosemary's hand. "I know the way. Let me guide you."

She led Rosemary down the stairs, hurrying past the door of the study. Thumps and crashes indicated a struggle still raged within. Florence did not dare stop and see who would be victorious. The fire had caught, and the wooden frame of Old House was alight. As they neared the door a beam gave way, sending a cascade of stone down that obstructed the doorway.

Florence turned towards the kitchen, only to see the floor licked by flame.

"No good." Rosemary coughed, sagging against Florence's shoulder. "Looks like this is it." She leaned her forehead against Florence's, shutting her eyes. "I'm so sorry I got you into this situation."

"You have nothing to be sorry for." Florence took a deep breath, steeling herself. A lifetime of fear was a hard habit to break. She hoisted Rosemary as if she lifted a child, and cradling her to her chest, walked through the burning hall.

The crackling of the flames filled her ears, their warmth restoring her skin to a semblance of life. Florence discovered she could still feel pain, as flames licked over her arms. She tightened her grip on Rosemary and kept moving, not allowing herself to think about what would happen if she failed.

A huge crash shook the house. Another wall had given way. Florence ran as fast as her skirts and her burden would allow. The door was just ahead.

She staggered into the night, dazed by the flames.

"This way." Julian grasped her arm. "We need to get away from the house."

Florence let him guide her across the grass. Rosemary hadn't stirred.

"I am very glad to see you, Miss Skelton." Julian continued. "I have to say that when I heard the hall collapse, I thought the worst."

"We're not out of danger yet." They were at the water's edge. Florence looked back and saw they were far enough from the house to have no fear of falling debris. She knelt, depositing Rosemary on the grass.

Rosemary coughed, opening soot-smudged eyes. "We're outside? Florence, you're a marvel."

"Don't talk. You'll injure your throat." Florence took the handkerchief and soaked it in water. She gave it back to Rosemary. "Are you burned?"

"Nothing that signifies. But you—" Rosemary's expression changed. She gasped, dismay plain on her face. "Your arm!"

Florence glanced down. Her sleeve was badly burned, the scorched fabric showing blistered skin beneath. "It's nothing."

"Nothing? Rabbit, that's—" Rosemary made to take her hand.

Julian placed his hand on hers, stopping her. "It's not polite to contradict a lady."

Florence gazed around, trying to orientate herself. The burning house illuminated their surroundings, but the night was pitch beyond, the bog a depthless hole. "The boat—you must find the boat."

"Us?" Rosemary staggered to her feet. Her hair had escaped its confines, and she was smudged with soot. One sleeve had torn away from the shoulder of her dress, and the rest of it was showing signs of its ill-treatment, but she looked as she had when defying the vicar: magnificent. The flames reflected in her eyes and gave her hair a copper sheen. "And what are you doing, rabbit? You're coming with us. We came here to rescue you."

"You came too late." Florence took a deep breath. "I'm very pleased to see you, so very pleased—but I cannot go with you." A crash resounded through the night as part of the roof gave way. Florence shut her eyes. She could say the words, but she could not bear to see Rosemary's reaction to them. "I'm not sure what happened. My memory is confused. I think… I think Mr Temple drowned me in the bog."

Rosemary placed a hand on her shoulder. "That's not possible."

"It's not possible," Florence repeated. "But it is. The woman who pulled me into the pond, she's Mrs Rutherford, Mr Temple's former secretary. Her body is at the museum in Hartlea. She's been dead for years—but I saw her at the lecture in Rotheram." She took a deep breath, continuing her tale. "These waters have a strange property. People who are placed in them, we—" She licked nerveless lips. "We don't stay dead."

She felt Rosemary's fingers tighten around her wrist. Searching for a pulse? Her laugh was unsteady. "I don't believe this. Your experiences have shaken you. This isn't true."

"But it is." Florence felt a tear roll down her cheek. She blinked it away, catching Rosemary's eyes. Instead of the revulsion she feared, Rosemary gazed at her, tenderness warring with a strange resolution.

"Listen." Rosemary's fingers tightened on her wrist. "I don't know what has happened to you, but we can do something about this. Julian's father is an expert in this sort of thing. We'll go back to Foxwood Court, consult him—"

"No!" Florence shrank back. See her family again—like this? "I can't! My father—"

"Miss Skelton is not going anywhere." Mrs Temple's voice rang out, cutting through the crackling flames. "And neither are the two of you."

She stood in the grass, hefting a wicked looking blade with the air of one familiar with its use. Margot stood at her side, armed with a bow.

Florence stepped in front of Julian and Rosemary, hoping she might act as a shield. "Mrs Temple is the guardian of the bogs. She has an uncanny sympathy with those confined to its waters." No sign of Graham. Presumably neither he, Mrs Rutherford nor Mr Temple had made it out of the house. Florence discovered that she harboured little regret over that fact.

A splash called their attention to the water—the policeman who had taken her statement at the railway station emerged from the water, and with him several people Florence didn't recognise. Villagers?

"More of Mrs Temple's friends?" Julian asked.

Rosemary pulled him away from the water's edge. "We're surrounded."

"This was not my intention," Mrs Temple said. "Ignatius forced my hand. But I promise you I will make it brief."

"No!" The thought of Rosemary and Julian sharing her fate was too much. Florence clenched her fists. "I will die before I let you take them."

Mrs Temple signalled Margot to raise her bow. "That boat has long sailed, my dear."

30

Florence lined herself up with Margot's bow, making sure she stood between her and her intended targets. She dared not turn her head, even as another splash indicated that the bog people were drawing closer. "Run, now—before they get on land. It's your best chance."

"And leave you?" Rosemary's hand tightened on Florence's arm.

"You can't save me." Florence saw Margot's fingers tighten on the bow, her expression implacable. Margot drew the bow. Florence shoved Rosemary towards the boatshed. "Run!"

The arrow did not hurt, but it knocked her backwards. Florence stumbled, losing her footing. Rosemary tugged at her, and she ran with Julian and Rosemary through the bog.

"This way!" Julian had found a trail. He did not hesitate, leading the way across the grass, avoiding soggy dead ends.

An arrow hit the ground at Florence's feet. She gritted her teeth and kept running.

The next arrow landed even wider. Too dark? They were running blindly now, only the sound of Julian's feet ahead guiding them through the bog.

An eerie howl split the night. Florence blundered to a halt. Were they running towards destruction? It sounded like the beast was just ahead of them!

"No time to explain." Rosemary grasped her hand, pulling her forward. "Julian's got a trick up his sleeve."

"That's not me," Julian's voice floated back to them.

Rosemary stilled. "What do you mean? Of course, it's you —" She trailed to a halt.

Lights bobbed in the marsh, drawing closer. This was not the meandering of the will-o'-the-wisp. This had purpose. Florence looked to her left and saw the water ripple with the approaching bog people. Ahead and to the right were the mysterious lights. Behind her, Mrs Temple and Margot were somewhere in the dark. "Trapped!" She couldn't contain her wail of dismay. It had come to this—failure!

"I'm not sure," Julian continued. "But it would be premature to abandon hope just yet, Miss Skelton. Rosemary told me to get help, and, well, I think this might be it." He raised his voice. "We're over here!"

A rough hand seized Florence's skirt. She stumbled, finding herself face to face with the policeman, using her skirt to haul himself from the water. She kicked him in his chest.

Rosemary punched him in the face in a way that was not ladylike, but very effective. He fell backwards into the water. "I don't know who Julian's summoned, but I'd rather take my chances with them than that lot behind us."

"Agreed." Florence scrambled back up the bank and ran towards the lights.

As they neared, they could see that the lights formed a procession headed their way. Soon, they could make out skirts, hats, and the glint of weaponry.

Florence's mouth fell open. "Miss Brickwell and the lepidopterist society!"

"You know them?" Rosemary sized up the approaching women.

"Not well. They're here to study the moths and butterflies of the swamp."

"They're very well armed to study butterflies." Rosemary nodded towards the crossbow that Miss Brickwell wielded. "Unless this swamp has even more surprises."

Julian stood very close to Florence and Rosemary, taking hold of their arms. He said nothing, but his eyes were wide.

Florence put an arm around him. She did not know if the lepidopterists were friends or foes, but if she could ease his worry, she would.

Miss Brickwell nodded to her. "Miss Skelton, it is a relief to see you again. When your father departed without you, we feared the worst."

"Yes, well." Florence's mind stalled. How had the lepidopterists known about that? "May I present my friends, Miss Scott and Master Westaway. We are anxious to return home—"

An arrow whizzed by them.

Miss Brickwell set down her lantern, aiming into the dark. Her vision was keener than Florence's. When she loosed her bolt, it met with a grunt, followed by the thud of a body hitting the ground. "Charmed. I am Miss Brickwell of the Lepidopterist Collective, and my colleagues, the Honourable Miss Fenley, Miss Barr and Miss Sarjent."

Miss Fenley loosed a bolt of her own. "Jolly pleased to meet you and all of that, but perhaps we should leave the full introductions until later? These swampy blighters seem rather insistent on making a nuisance of themselves."

Jemima's military-style ammunition belt looked very odd paired with her bonnet. She beckoned Florence and her friends towards her. "You can find your way through the bog, Master Westaway? Go. We'll cover you."

"And leave you?" Florence was dismayed. "You don't know what you face—these are no ordinary people."

"We did get that impression," Miss Sarjent stood side by side with Miss Brickwell and Miss Fenley. No matter how many bolts they loosed into the dark, the bog people drew closer. They were visible now.

"Let us help." Rosemary snatched up a bow, aiming it at the nearest of the advancing bog people. The bolt she fired connected with its target, sending the man stumbling back a few paces. In a matter of seconds, he righted himself and continued stalking towards them.

Florence stepped back, pulling Julian with her. "They're dead. They don't feel pain."

"I thought they were jolly persistent." Miss Fenley lowered her crossbow. "A change in plan—" In her moment of distraction, Margot loomed up out of the water, seizing her ankle. Miss Fenley, caught off balance, plunged into the water.

"Pat!" Miss Barr screamed, diving after her. Miss Sarjent flung herself on Margot, wrestling her to the ground.

This meant that only Rosemary and Miss Brickwell maintained their defences. The bog people drew closer. As Julian hefted Miss Sarjent's dropped crossbow, Florence cast around for some way to help.

Miss Brickwell's lantern sat on the grass.

Florence stared at it. She'd said the bog people did not feel pain. She had felt nothing when she'd fallen from the attic window. But making her way through the flames, that had stung.

Could fire be the bog people's weakness? There was only one way to find out. Florence gripped the lantern by the handle. She spotted Mrs Temple in the rear, brandishing her sword as she urged her followers forward. Florence spun around, building momentum, and heaved the lantern through the air. *Lord, please let this work—*

By pure fluke, the lantern connected with Mrs Temple, spilling oil and flames over her. In a moment, she was alight. The bog people nearest her turned to help.

"Interesting strategy, Miss Skelton, but short lived, I fear." Miss Brickwell paused a moment. "Surrounded as we are by water, fire will not give us much of an advantage."

Florence's heart sank. Miss Brickwell was right. Even as she watched, Mrs Temple plunged into the blog. She surfaced, her flames extinguished, turning baleful eyes upon Florence. The bog people that surrounded her turned their gazes to her as one.

Florence knew the meaning in that gaze. She was their next victim. She stepped back.

Miss Barr pulled herself out of the water, turning to assist Miss Sarjent onto the bank. "If I'm not mistaken, Miss Skelton might be onto something. This marsh contains almost as much gas as water—"

A sudden almighty boom filled the air, throwing Florence to the ground. "What—" She picked herself up, gasping at the sight.

Hell on earth could not be more terrible than this. The bog burned, flames jumping from one patch of grass to another. Further ignitions followed as the pockets of gas within the marsh caught alight.

"To me!" Mrs Temple turned, plunging back into the bog. She seemed to be trying to outrun the flames, heading back toward Old House. "We must protect the burial site."

The remaining bog people turned after her. One didn't rise, destroyed by the flame.

"Do we pursue?" Miss Sarjent levelled her crossbow at a retreating bog-person's back.

"No," Miss Brickwell said. "Our primary responsibility is to get our guests to safety. We're none of us impervious to flame."

The fire licked closer to them, too. Florence stepped back.

"In that case, I move we run." Miss Barr jerked her head in what Florence guessed was the direction of their cottage.

"Seconded." Miss Fenley took off across the grass. Rosemary, Florence, and Julian ran after the lepidopterists. The crackle of flames behind them kept them moving at a fast pace. A succession of small booms indicated they were still in danger.

"There!" The cottage was ahead of them. Instead of heading inside, the lepidopterists made as one for the shore. Florence, Rosemary and Julian were shepherded into a boat, and Miss Brickwell and Miss Fenley assumed the oars, as Miss Barr and Miss Sarjent shoved off.

In a matter of seconds, they were pulling out into the channel that cut through the bog.

"Not a moment too soon," Miss Barr said. "Look!" The cottage roof had caught.

"My new hat is in there," Miss Sarjent mourned. "Only worn twice."

"I'm sorry." Florence hung her head, staring at the bottom of the boat. "This is my fault. If I hadn't thrown the lantern—"

"And saved all our lives?" Rosemary squeezed her hand. "You've got nothing to be sorry for, rabbit."

Florence shook her head. "The lady at the pond. That was a warning. She wanted me to stay away. If I'd listened, if I'd never come to Aylesport, none of us would be in this predicament."

"If you hadn't come to Aylesport, Mr Temple might have claimed another victim—one far less prepared to defend herself." Miss Brickwell nodded to Miss Barr, who took her place at the oar. She seated herself in front of Rosemary, Florence, and Julian. "The time has come to be open with you, Miss Skelton. We are no ordinary lepidopterists. We had heard rumours of strange activity in the bog and, coupled with the find of the mysterious bog woman body, we decided we should come to Aylesport to investigate. Our investigation had stalled until Miss Skelton's arrival precipitated things."

Wait... was that a good thing or a bad? Florence swallowed. "Oh."

Rosemary narrowed her eyes at Miss Brickwell. "If you're not ordinary lepidopterists, what are you?" she asked. "And what gives you the right to go around investigating willy-nilly?"

Miss Brickwell opened her mouth, but the answer came from an unexpected source.

"Can't you tell?" Julian said. His eyes caught the light of the flames, glowing yellow. "They're werewolves."

31

"Now this is more like it." Miss Barr surveyed the table in front of them with satisfaction. They'd pushed two tables in the station cafe in Castleford together, and the table was now heaped with fresh scones, a pot of jam, and a generous bowl of cream.

Miss Brickwell lifted the teapot. "Miss Skelton, may I interest you in a cup of tea?"

So much had happened in so short a time that Florence's mind still spun with it all. It was a relief to have a question she could answer. "Yes, please. Milk, but not sugar."

Miss Brickwell poured tea as she did everything else: efficiently. "Miss Scott?"

"The same as Flo—Miss Skelton, please."

Florence glanced up. Rosemary avoided her eye, but there was colour in her cheeks. She dropped her own gaze to her cup of tea. Did Rosemary—despite everything—still think of her as Florence?

"Just milk for you." Miss Sarjent filled Julian's cup.

"I drink tea at home," he protested.

She wagged her finger at him. "You're a growing pup. This stuff stunts your growth."

Julian—a werewolf. As were the lepidopterists. Florence shook her head. She still could not believe it. "What happens now?"

"First, we will escort you back to Foxwood Court." Miss Fenley buttered herself a scone. "From the sounds of things, this Leighton chap is the sort of fellow we should know."

"He certainly is." Rosemary pursed her lips. "How long have you been…"

"Lepidopterists?" Miss Barr's eyes sparkled with amusement. "Pat and Brick are born wolves. I was bitten at my coming out party—the nerve! Honestly! I still can't believe it."

"I contracted it from my former fiancé." Miss Sarjent said.

"Former fiancé?" Florence repeated. "I'm sorry."

Miss Sarjent pursed her lips. "I'm better off without him."

"Hear, hear." Miss Fenley slapped the table. "The male werewolf is the worst—present company excepted, Master Westaway."

Julian tilted his head. "Where are the male werewolves?"

"Off somewhere having a pity party that they call the Society of Keepers," Miss Brickwell snorted. "Ridiculous."

"Some noble idiot had the idea that lycanthropy was a curse on no account to be handed down to the next generation," Miss Fenley explained. "So, he instigated the policy that male werewolves self-segregate, shunning all female-companionship—us, especially."

"Did it occur to them to consult us? Or that we might have thoughts on the matter?" Miss Barr rolled her eyes. "No, not them!"

"What are we to do?" Miss Brickwell said. "A woman's only career in life is matrimony and motherhood, and we are cast off from both."

"Do we martyr ourselves? Sit around languishing, casting melting looks at the objects of our unrequited affection?"

Miss Barr heaved a sigh that would have been more convincing, had she not clotted cream on her chin.

"Do we hell!" chorused Miss Sarjent and Miss Fenley as one.

Miss Brickwell smirked, her manner that of a schoolteacher with precocious students. "We do not. Since the roles dictated by society are beyond us, we have said a quiet but firm farewell to its dictates and formed a community of our own."

"We support each other, taking mutual responsibility for the nights of the month where we are indisposed," Miss Sarjent placed a buttered scone in front of Julian. "Eat up. You've had a long night."

"Lepidoptera is a convenient cover for our activities," Miss Brickwell continued. "There are moths and butterflies everywhere, and one only has to be tolerably familiar to convince the average member of the public."

"You convinced me." Florence pursed her lips. "How do you fund your activities?"

"A number of us come from money. Miss Fenley, for instance. She's got a sizeable allowance."

Miss Fenley grimaced. "I donate most of it to the collective."

"We receive quite a few bequests and marriage settlements. We also have a few enterprises, for those who have an interest in farming or business." Miss Brickwell nodded. "And we campaign for women's suffrage, better education, and we organise lectures and other such educational evenings for our members."

"It sounds wonderful," Rosemary breathed. "Do you only admit w—lepidopterists as members?"

"Usually, yes. But I think the board would consider an application from you and Miss Skelton, considering Miss Skelton's…unique circumstances."

If blushing had still been possible, Florence would have

been bright red. At least being dead has this much for it: she did not broadcast her embarrassment so plainly. "I should like to be considered."

Florence sipped her tea, savouring its warmth. Once they'd reached the train station, the lepidopterist had commandeered a carriage and set to work restoring their complexions, hair and dresses from the ravages of the night. Florence's icy hands and lack of colour had not gone unremarked on for long. She'd confessed to being one of the bog people. Instead of the revulsion she'd expected, the lepidopterists insisted she remain with their party.

Rosemary's hand grasped hers beneath the table. She gave Florence a smile. "As would I."

Had Rosemary forgotten their quarrel? Florence squeezed her hand. She must find an opportunity to talk to Rosemary alone. "Miss Scott, would you care to—"

"Is that the time?" Miss Brickwell stood. "We've got to catch our next train."

In all the bustle of travel, Florence didn't get the chance to speak to Rosemary alone. Miss Sarjent said goodbye to them at King's Cross, continuing to London where she would report to the 'higher ups' on the events in Aylesport. The rest of them continued to Rotheram where they alighted, hiring a carriage to take them the rest of the way to Foxwood Court.

Florence sat in the centre of the carriage with Miss Barr's cloak pulled up over her head, Rosemary on one side, Miss Brickwell on the other. Her stomach churned with each familiar sight. Home—but it was not her home any longer.

Rosemary threaded her fingers through Florence's. "I cannot tell you how much it means to have you back at last. If only the circumstances were different!"

"Do you think Lord Cross will be furious?" Florence pulled the cloak tighter around herself. "I know how much he values his privacy."

"He may be annoyed at first," Julian assured her. "But once he hears your story, I'm sure he will be most interested —and very pleased to meet the rest of you."

The lepidopterists seemed to know when they reached the boundary of Foxwood Park.

"This is your territory? Not bad for a scrap of a kid." Miss Barr stood to get a better view of the park.

Miss Fenley tugged her skirts to get her to sit down. "Good hunting?"

A hesitant smile flickered across Julian's face. "Yes— although the gamekeeper does not approve."

Miss Fenley snorted. "They often don't."

It seemed like only a handful of minutes before they stood in the grand entranceway, a bewildered manservant offering to take their cloaks.

Florence shrank back. She could not be recognised. If her family knew she was there!

Julian took her hand. "They're usually in the library at this hour," he said. "This way."

He led the way into the library. "Good morning, Father, Lord Cross. We have some visitors."

"Julian!" Mr Leighton scrambled to his feet, dashing across the room with more haste than was proper. He flung his arms around his son. "Don't ever run off like that again! Do you know how worried we have been?"

"It was my fault," Miss Scott said. "I could not stand by and abandon Miss Skelton to her fate, and I thought it likely I'd need assistance."

"Miss Skelton?" Lord Cross peered at her. "I understood that you were in London pursuing a literary career."

"Lies." Rosemary clenched her fists. "As I told you, Miss Skelton was doing no such thing! While her father thought her absconding, Florence was Mr Temple's latest victim."

"Victim?" Mr Leighton looked up from his examination of his son. "Are you injured, Miss Skelton?"

"It's worse than that, Mr Leighton." Florence looked behind her to check that the door was closed. The three lepidopterists waited, their eyes weighing Lord Cross and Mr Leighton.

Florence took a deep breath. It was one thing to tell her friends—quite another to tell Lord Cross and Mr Leighton! They could have her committed to an asylum—or even worse, a mortuary!

A movement drew her gaze to Rosemary, who had crossed her arms. Her gaze rested on Florence, her expression expectant.

Rosemary had no doubts about Florence's ability to meet the situation. Florence discovered her own fears dissipating. "I'm not injured, exactly. I'm dead."

"Dead?" Lord Cross exchanged a sharp glance with Mr Leighton. "This is no time to joke, Miss Skelton. Your father is very concerned for you."

"Listen to her story," Julian said. "You'll see."

"Let us reserve judgement." Mr Leighton drew a chair up to the fire and motioned Florence towards it. "I imagine you have quite the story to share with us, Miss Skelton."

Florence inclined her head, taking the seat. The warmth of the fire was nothing to Rosemary's regard. She felt renewed strength flood her veins. "That I do. I suppose it starts with the woman in the pond—the woman I saw at Mr Temple's lecture."

Lord Cross and Mr Leighton listened to Florence's story without interrupting. Her credibility was helped by the arrival of a telegram from Mr Scott, indicating that he and Dawson had arrived at Aylesport only to find Old House in smoking ruins, and Miss Skelton's body in the bog.

"Tell them to keep looking," Florence said. "Mr Vaugham's body is there too. I heard Mr Temple hide his body in the water—no doubt trusting the coldness of the bog to preserve him until he could prepare a suitable location to 'find' him."

Mr Leighton shook his head. "Even having felt your lack of pulse for myself, I find it hard to take in. And Mr Vaugham too—he must have been dead the entire time he was in Foxwood, and we had no idea!"

Florence's head whipped up. "Mr Vaugham was here?"

Mr Leighton nodded. "He brought your message to your father. Mr Skelton thought Mr Vaugham's story was very odd, so he brought him to visit us so that we could discuss the matter."

Florence pressed a hand to her forehead. Was she happy Vaugham had, in some manner, survived; or sorry that he shared her fate? Did he know what had happened? And where was he now?

Lord Cross frowned. "It is not a pleasant feeling to know that one has hosted a murderer. If our hospitality played any role in your decision to accept Mr Temple's offer of employment, Miss Skelton—"

Florence held her hand up, forestalling him. "He was my father's school friend. That was recommendation enough." Only then did she realise that she'd interrupted a Lord. "I beg your pardon."

No one else seemed to have noticed anything strange in her behaviour. "I'll let Mr Scott know," Lord Cross said. "A search must be made for Mr Vaugham."

"Already on it," Miss Barr sprawled in front of the fire. "Jackie will have reached London by now and made her report. The collective is on it."

Lord Cross raised his eyebrows at her response—or perhaps it was the rapidity with which Miss Burr had made herself at home on his rug? He exchanged a glance with Mr Leighton and walked out of the library.

Mr Leighton winced. "Perhaps you'd be more comfortable on the sofa, Miss Burr?"

"No. I'm quite comfortable here."

"Oh sit up, Jemima." Miss Brickwell ordered. "You must set a good example for Master Westaway."

Julian watched Miss Fenley make quick work of the cucumber sandwiches. "I lie on the rug all the time."

His father elbowed him. "Not when we have company." Mr Leighton's eyes gleamed as they rested on the lepidopterists. "I am fascinated by the little I have heard of your society. Anything you care to tell us would be useful, not simply from the matter of Julian's future, but as a student of the phasmatological…"

Miss Brickwell bared very sharp teeth in an amused grin. "I think we have a lot to talk about, Mr Leighton."

The subject would occupy them for some time. Florence set aside her cup of tea. "May I be excused? I should like to rest." She wasn't tired, not exactly, but she needed silence to collect her thoughts.

"I shall let Surplis know to show you to your room." Mr Leighton made to reach for the bell pull.

"No!" Florence faltered. "I can't be recognised. It is only a matter of time before news of my demise reaches Foxwood. When that happens—"

"I see your point." Mr Leighton frowned. "Servants are very nervy about such things."

Rosemary linked her arm through Florence's. "You'll stay in my room. Come on."

Florence pulled the hood of her cloak up over her head and let Rosemary lead her upstairs. Her skin was warm where Rosemary's arm rested against hers. Florence felt something flutter in the vicinity of her heart. Perhaps she was not fully dead?

"Here." Rosemary's room was on the third floor in what had once been a nursery. The room was plainly furnished with a desk, bookcase, and a bed in one room, and a second bed and Rosemary's wardrobe and washstand in the adjoining attendant's room. "I hope you don't mind that it's not as fancy as the other rooms. I wanted somewhere that I could think and work—somewhere that felt real."

Florence glanced over the papers on the desk. She recognised more than one sketch of Carmilla. "I think it lovely."

Rosemary's jaw tightened as she faced Florence, her fists clenching. "I know you want rest, so I won't be long—but I must say this."

Florence snatched her hand away from the papers, heart thumping with alarm.

Rosemary thrust her chin into the air. "I had no right to ignore your wishes and send your manuscript away—none. I told myself I was acting for your benefit, but you were right. I was using you for my own ends."

Florence felt her shoulders sag with relief. Did Rosemary still want to be friends with her? "You were right to call me a coward. I feared so much to lose my family's approval. I did not see that something so easily lost was not worth the value I gave it."

"Don't say that." Rosemary's voice was harsh. "Don't you see? You were alive when your father visited Old House. He might have saved—you might have escaped. But he found the letter from the publisher in your room, and that convinced him you'd run away. If it hadn't been for my presumption—if I hadn't been so selfish—you..." She half-gasped, half sobbed. "You'd be alive now. Oh, Florence—" Rosemary wept. Beautiful, invincible, powerful Rosemary wept.

Florence stared. All this time—the entirety of their journey back to Foxwood, had Rosemary been holding this inside? She'd never seen grief so powerful. Rosemary's sobs shook her entire body. "Rosemary!" Florence stepped forward, folding the other woman in her arms. "It's all right. I'm here now—you came back. You found me, brought me here—you came back for me when my family didn't."

"Because of me." Rosemary's grief did not seem likely to abate soon. "I was so stupid—so selfish—"

Florence gathered her arms more tightly around Rosemary, stroking her arm. "Don't speak of it again." She pressed her lips to Rosemary's cheek. "You came back for me. More than that—you saved me."

She felt Rosemary still in her arms, her sobs fading to a shudder. Florence stroked her hair. How strange to be the one giving comfort when it was Rosemary who so inspired her. "There were so many times I was afraid, so many times where my courage failed me and I thought this is it—I can no longer go on. Every time I gave up, your memory came to me —your strength. It was your courage that sustained me through the ordeal, Rosemary—your courage that sustains me now."

Rosemary's chest heaved with the after-effects of her grief. "Nonsense. Carmilla—the mind that imagined her feats must possess nerves of steel."

Florence wiped the tears from Rosemary's eyes, tipping her face up to meet hers. "Didn't you guess? Carmilla is you." Had she thought herself spared from blushing? No—in Rosemary's proximity, her skin flooded red, just as it had when she was alive. "You didn't simply save my life. You showed me life and gave me the courage to pursue it."

"Florence. You don't—loathe me?" Rosemary peered at her.

"I could never." Florence hesitated. "I thought you despised me."

"Not for one second." Rosemary's grip tightened on Florence's arm. "If I was angry, it was because you'd shown me as the thoughtless, impetuous beast that I am. What is my bravado and bluster next to your innate goodness and inner fortitude?"

Rosemary thought her brave? Florence found it easier to gather her courage. "My circumstances are strange. I am in more need of a friend than ever. Rosemary—"

"Yes."

Florence blinked. "You do not know what I was about to propose."

"The resumption of our friendship?" Rosemary's eyes were red-rimmed but her glance arch.

Florence felt herself smile for the first time since her demise. "Nothing would make me happier."

Rosemary folded her in a tight hug. "My heart, my life, is yours, rabbit. Yours." She leaned in, pressing her lips to Florence's.

Kissing, too, brought life back to her skin. Florence tasted the salt of Rosemary's tears, breathed in her warmth. When

Rosemary pulled away, Florence needed to steady herself against the back of the armchair. "Oh."

Rosemary peered at her. "Did I presume too much?"

"N-no." Florence swallowed. "Perhaps. But in a good way." If the heat in her cheeks was any sign, she was a veritable bonfire. "We, too, have much to talk about."

EPILOGUE

Mrs Skelton, her eyes red-rimmed and her complexion a trifle paler than usual, answered the vicarage door. She dropped Pip and Cross a low curtsey. "It is kind of you to think of us. And kind indeed of you to offer your help with the arrangements."

No matter what he thought of Mrs Skelton otherwise, her grief was genuine. Pip stepped forward, taking her hand in his. "It is the least we can do. To lose a daughter so young…"

Mrs Skelton pressed her handkerchief to her lips. The tremor passed. She was in control of herself once more. "She is at peace and, I trust, with the Lord. Would you care to see her?" Without waiting for a reply, she led them into the best drawing room.

The coffin lay open on the table. Miss Skelton lay within, dressed in her best muslin, hair combed until it shone. She looked as though she slept, were it not for the lilies placed on her breast, undisturbed by any breath.

"She looks beautiful, doesn't she?" Mrs Skelton spoke with quiet satisfaction. "That's some consolation at least. You would never know she was—" Her voice faltered. "She—" Mrs Skelton turned and walked out of the room.

This was the most awkward viewing he'd ever attended. Pip exchanged a look with Cross. He stepped forward to inspect Miss Skelton.

There was no sign of her unnatural death, no indication of her unnatural afterlife. She looked like a young woman snatched from life—albeit a well-preserved young woman.

"Strange to think that even now, Miss Skelton is sitting in the nursery, no doubt having morning tea with Julian."

"Hush." Cross tilted his head towards the closed door. The murmur of voices beyond indicated they were not the vicarage's only visitors. He held his hat in hand, stepping forward to look down at Miss Skelton. "A unique young woman, in more ways than one." He bowed his head and motioned Pip towards the door.

Respects paid, Pip stepped into the Skelton's parlour, where a group of village women imbibed vast amounts of tea. They greeted Pip's appearance with a great deal of adjusting of their shawls and gloves. Pip suppressed his grimace, returning the greetings. That he was Lord Cross's heir was widely known. The neighbourhood considered him not so confirmed a bachelor as Lord Cross. Quite a few of Foxwood's female population aimed at him. "A terrible tragedy, isn't it? What a sad loss to the Skeltons—to our community."

Hannah flitted about the group, refilling teacups and removing empty plates. Cross coughed, approaching her. "Miss Skelton? They found this letter among your sister's belongings. It appears to have been intended for you."

Hannah bowed her head, accepting the letter. "Thank you, Lord Cross. This means much."

"Is your father receiving visitors?"

She shook her head. "I believe he is working on his sermon. He has a lot to prepare."

"Our carriage and horses are at his disposal for the funeral parade should he wish." Cross gave Miss Skelton a bow and the remaining women a brief nod. "Come, Leighton."

Pip breathed out as they dismounted the carriage, climbing the steps of Foxwood Court. "I am glad that's over. I was so worried I'd let something slip!"

"We're not out of the woods yet," Cross murmured, looking ahead.

Surplis waited in the hall. He bowed as they approached. "Welcome home, Lord Cross, Mr Leighton. I trust that your call of duty went well?"

"As well as it could." Cross handed Surplis his hat and began shrugging out of his coat. "I have put our stables at the Skelton's disposal."

"Very good sir."

Pip, halfway out of his jacket, sniffed. Cigar smoke? "Do we have other guests?"

Surplis coughed. "The lepidopterists wished to teach Master Julian how to play at billiards and asked for some refreshments. I offered them the Turkish cigarettes we keep for Dr Goodfellow's visits, but one of the young ladies requested something stronger. I offered them your lordship's cigars."

Cross blinked. "My cigars?"

"They appear to have found them very satisfactory."

Judging from the amount of smoke in the hall, they had indeed enjoyed the cigars immensely. "How very modern. Does Julian appear to enjoy billiards?"

"It is sometimes hard to judge Master Julian's opinion, but when I refreshed their drinks, I heard Miss Brickwell complimenting him on his mastery of the draw shot."

Probably all right. "We won't disturb them." Pip nudged Cross.

He scowled in the direction of the billiard room. "You've done very well, Surplis."

The butler took Pip's coat and hat. "Miss Scott and the

young lady with so remarkable a resemblance to the late Miss Skelton are in the library and desirous of speaking to you."

Pip schooled his expression blank.

"Is that so?" Cross said blandly. "Then we shall see them at once."

Surplis bowed, sailing off to the coatroom.

Pip looked after him. "Is that Surplis's way of telling us we're not as subtle as we think we are?"

"No doubt." Cross rested a hand on Pip's shoulder. "Let's see what the young ladies have to say."

Miss Scott and Miss Skelton sat in conversation by the fire. They looked up as the gentlemen entered. Pip was struck by the glow in each of their eyes. Far from being prepared for a funeral, the pair looked as though they had hit upon some novel new pastime.

"Good morning, Miss Scott, Miss Skelton."

"Miss Eyre, if you please." Miss Skelton tucked a ringlet behind one ear. To make her less recognisable, the lepidopterists had contrived to make her straight hair curl and found her a new dress. "I must get accustomed to my new name."

"Of course, Miss Eyre." Cross drew a seat up to join them. "Your family appears to be bearing your loss with due fortitude. I delivered your letter to your sister."

Miss Skelton bowed her head. "Thank you. It means much to say goodbye to Hannah."

Miss Scott placed her hand over Miss Skelton's. "Miss Eyre has a request to make."

She blushed, her shoulders tensing. "This will no doubt sound very presumptuous, Lord Cross, Mr Leighton, but you know my circumstances, so I hope you will give me some indulgence. I have limited friends to whom I can apply for help." Miss Skelton's eyes were downcast. "I ask for a loan."

"A loan?" Cross leaned forward. "You have come to a decision regarding your future."

Miss Skelton nodded. "I cannot stay in Foxwood. I have had an offer of publication for a book. The loan would allow us to travel to London and find accommodation while we wait for the Lepidopterist Collective to review our application for membership."

"We?" Pip turned to Miss Scott. "Am I to infer that you are leaving us, too, Miss Scott?"

"I said I'd stay only until I found another job." Miss Scott raised her chin, as if expecting him to argue with her. "I will edit and illustrate Florence's stories and perhaps do some illustrations for magazines."

"Most suitable," Pip said. One did not argue with Miss Scott if one could avoid it. "I can think of no better employment for both of you."

"I could pay you back once I receive my advance from the publisher," Miss Skelton continued. "I should not need the loan long."

Cross stroked his beard. "What does Mr Scott think of your decision?"

"He is sorry to see me leave Foxwood but cheered by the notion we are only going so far as London." Miss Scott's grin for a moment reflected that of her brother's: wry. "I suspect Julian's future will involve a lot of trips to London for the museums and galleries."

"There are worse things than introducing a boy to a bit of culture," Pip said.

Cross met his glance and nodded. "How much do you think you'll need? I'll make you out a cheque now."

The cheque was written, and the young ladies departed, but Pip made no move towards his desk. "It won't be too long before Julian will also leave us to make his way in the world."

Cross glanced down at him. "We have a few years yet.

Miss Scott was the impetus behind his removal to Aylesport—"

Pip waved the protest aside. "It's the presence of the lepidopterists. I always knew that Julian would meet others of his kind, but I didn't think it would happen so soon."

Cross pulled his chair up next to Pip. "You are concerned?"

Pip grimaced. "Yes—concerned he might prefer their company. And jealous—which is ridiculous. And all manner of things beside." He shook his head. "Who would have thought fatherhood would be so hard?"

Cross's smile was tender. He reached out, stroking Pip's cheek. "Julian adores you. No matter what happens, that won't change. And I—"

The door creaked as it was opened. Cross snatched his hand back.

Julian stepped into the doorway, his cheeks suffused with a glow of pleasure. "Father, Miss Brickwell says I am not the worst billiards player she has ever seen, and Miss Fenley says that I'm a good egg. Do you think that a compliment?"

Julian's timing still left much to be desired. Pip patted the seat next to him. "I should think so. Were there any contextual clues?"

"I had given her my handkerchief." Julian sat down.

"Then yes, I should say that was a compliment." Pip pursed his lips as he watched his son, considering the question he both wanted and feared to ask.

"Miss Barr said that she would ask if I can be an honorary lepidopterist," Julian continued. "They don't usually let boys into their collective, but she said that we're unique enough that they might just bend the rules."

"I don't think—" Pip paused. "Wait. Did you say 'we'?"

Julian nodded. "Miss Brickwell thinks you and Lord Cross would make excellent members." He paused, adding with a diffidence that was unconvincing, "That is, assuming you're interested."

Pip met Cross's eyes. He nodded, his gaze amused. Pip had to fight his own answering smile. To Julian, this was very serious. "Do you want to be a lepidopterist, Julian?"

"Very much."

"Then you may tell Miss Brickwell that Lord Cross and I would be happy to discuss becoming honorary lepidopterists, also."

"Thank you, Father." Julian squeezed him. "And other father." He gave Cross a quick hug. "I will tell her right now."

Cross snorted as the door shut behind Julian. "Lepidopterists—at our age!"

"It's never too late to pick up a new interest." Pip did his best to keep his tone casual. "Speaking of new things, with Miss Scott gone, I shall need a new curator for my collection."

From the glance Cross sent him, he was no more successful at hiding his intentions than Julian. "You have someone in mind?"

Pip tugged at his collar. "Mr Vaugham has suitable historic background and will be at a loose end right now. I can think of no one better suited."

"No one better suited for you to investigate, you mean." Cross stroked his beard. "Well, we were due a trip to London. And as Miss Scott said, Julian could do with some culture. You may as well begin your investigations there."

Cross knew him too well—and Pip could not be better pleased. "I'll make the arrangements at once."

Look what the mailman dragged in…

Jasper Carruthers has turned deciphering smudged addresses and avoiding conflict into a fine art. A crate from Egypt contains a problem he cannot return to sender: a mummified cat sought by a desperate thief. Failure to deliver the cat will give the Postmaster General—Jasper's vengeful son—the excuse he needs to oust Jasper from the postal service.

Jasper's attempts to deliver the package attract the interest of Captain Candy, an insufferable bore under the mistaken impression that Jasper tolerates him. Even worse: the cat does not seem to realise she's dead. Jasper's not sure if he needs an Egyptologist or an exorcist. There's only one thing he's certain of: he needs help.

Forced to trust Candy with his secret, Jasper may at last have found something worth fighting for—but can he deliver the package before the cat lets herself out of the bag?

The Dead Letter Office is book twelve in the Read by Candlelight series of standalone Gothic novellas featuring an expanding cast of LGBTQIA+ characters. Pairs well with a hot pot of tea and a biscuit.

To be first to read *The Dead Letter Office*, support me on Patreon. Alternatively, you can preorder it on Amazon. Stay up to date with my news and future releases by signing up to my newsletter.

THE WING COMMANDER'S CURSE

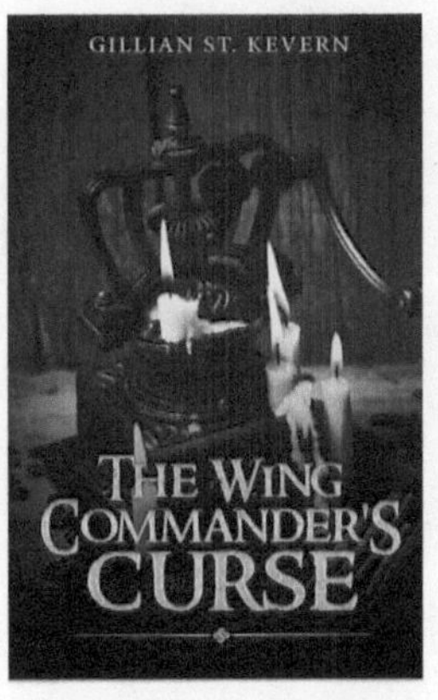

An unbreakable curse.
England overrun by monsters.
Two men locked in a losing battle.

England, 1915.

Jonah Valliant longs for active service, but is stuck making coffee for the local officers. A year ago, the world erupted into magical chaos. No one knows why Britain is overrun by fearsome worms, magical creatures whose gaze turns men to stone, or how to stop them. When Jonah loses his temper with Wing Commander Mallory, he has no idea that picking a quarrel with the wizard may lead to Britain's salvation–or its destruction.

Augustus Mallory carries more than the weight of the war effort on his shoulders. He's the last of the Mallory wizards, feared for their power, arrogance and the dark family curse. Losing his heart to Jonah endangers everything Mallory cares about, but Jonah may possess the key to defeating the worms once and for all. Mallory's only hope: staving off his doom long enough to learn the dreadful truth behind the Quickening.

Sign up to my newsletter for your free copy of The Wing Commander's Curse.

BOOK REC: MISE EN DEATH: A LEBEAU CHOCOLATES ADVENTURE

I confess that I have not read this yet, but it is top of my reading list. When life gets too crazy or overwhelming, cozy mysteries are my go-to… And a cozy mystery featuring a chocolatier as the main character? Yeah, I'm all about this.

ALEX LEBEAU, CHOCOLATIER AND CHEF INSTRUC-TOR, wants nothing more than to give her almost grown son a quiet life and a place to call home. Settling in Honfleur, Louisiana, Alex can distance herself from her chaotic romantic past and association with the clandestine group Bellicose Solanum (BelSol).

Things might be looking up for her when she takes a job at a promising cooking school. Her contentment is short-lived when a famous millionaire of Honfleur is murdered during the school's catering event on an airship.

As the body count begins to rise in an eccentric series of mishaps, all evidence points to one of her most beloved culinary students—her son.

If word gets out about the murder, the culinary school's reputation is ruined, but most importantly Alex cannot let her son be found guilty for a crime he didn't commit.

With the help of Josephine, the school potager and voice of reason, Alex hesitantly rallies up old friends from her checkered past to help clear her son's name.

Armed with the fortune that might (or might not) favor the brave, Alex and Josephine race to find the killer before those nearest to Alex become the latest victims.

Taste test Mise en Death on Amazon today.

ACKNOWLEDGMENTS

Very special thanks to my Patreon supporters for their continued encouragement: Jennifer, Julia, Kathleen, Khadija, Lexy, Patricia, SpookMouse, Theanna and Y Lee—you rock! Thank you! A warm welcome to new patron Wiebke—nice to have you with us!

Another big thank you to Anne and Sera for reading and keeping me on track, and Emma B's editorial magic. I'd also like to thank Kevin for his expert proofreading assistance—your help is greatly appreciated. Another big thank you to the Christchurch chapter of the Romance Writers of New Zealand for commiserating with me when I had to delete 17,000 words and start my draft again... Your sympathy meant a lot!

ABOUT THE AUTHOR

I realised I wanted to be an author when, as a teenager, I found myself getting annoyed that the characters in the books I read weren't doing what I wanted them to do. Now that I'm a writer, they still don't.

I write a variety of genres, ranging from short and silly contemporary romances to urban fantasy and mystery. My current project is the *Read by Candlelight* series of gothic romances inspired by the works of M R James, J S Le Fanu and the Brontë sisters.

In my non-writing life, I live in my native New Zealand, where I enjoy flat whites, playing pretend with my niece and nephew and trying to keep up with my ever increasing to be read pile. I'm the co-founder of the New Zealand Rainbow Romance Writers.

If you enjoyed *The Lady of the Bog* and want to leave a review, I will be so overjoyed, I may spill my tea.

gillianstkevern.com
info@gillianstkevern.com

CHARACTER GLOSSARY

Suggested by Barb, this is a quick glossary of characters intended to counteract the confusion caused by the fact that the Read by Candlelight series is written and published out of chronological order. This is a work in progress as I intend to update this as I go rather than do it all at once. This is written to accompany *The Lady of the Bog*, and further characters will be added as I have the chance. Get the most up to date version online.

Character Glossary.

Cross, Thomas, Lord of Foxwood.

Landowner of Foxwood Court and much of the surrounding countryside. A man of uncertain temper, wide correspondence, and a tragic past. Pip's employer and Julian's guardian. First appearance: The Secretary and the Ghost.

Dawson, Francis.

An artist, currently employed by Pip as an art teacher for Julian. Known for the meticulous care he gives his moustache and his work, and the indifference he displays towards pretty much everything. First appearance: <u>The Art of Drowning.</u>

Goodfellow, Harriet.

A no-nonsense woman with a practical bent, Harriet has proven herself as Foxwood's doctor many times over. No patience for those who believe a woman incapable of working just as well as a man. First appearance: <u>The Secretary and the Ghost.</u>

Leighton, Phillip (Pip).

Secretary and heir to Lord Cross, enthusiastic amateur phasmatologist and investigator of the occult. Indifferent health, trained as a legal clerk. Julian's adoptive father. First appearance: <u>The Secretary and the Ghost.</u>

Scott, Basil.

An affable man. Currently employed by Pip as a tutor for Julian. Previously worked as a school teacher and as a consular assistant in Italy. Well travelled, has an abiding love of music. Good friends with Francis Dawson, has one sister: Rosemary. First appearance: <u>The Weeping Statue.</u>

Scott, Rosemary.

A spirited young woman with very definite thoughts on freedom and woman's rights. A farmer's daughter, she is now adjusting to an entirely new way of life. First appearance: <u>The Worst Behaved Werewolf.</u>

Skelton, Florence.

The daughter of Foxwood's vicar, Horace Skelton. A meek young woman with a love of literature, in particular, Jane Eyre. Takes a job as secretary. First appearance: The Lady of the Bog.

Skelton, Horace.

Replaced Gladwell as vicar to Foxwood. A stern man with a strict bent, a terror to choir boys. Disapproves of Pip's interest in the supernatural. First appearance: The Lady of the Bog.

Vaugham, Amit.

Adopted son of a British Missionary. Vaugham's ambition is to become a respected historian. First appearance: The Lady of the Bog.

Westaway, Julian.

Adopted son of Pip, ward of Lord Cross, Patrick O'Connor's godson. Defies explanation. First appearance: <u>The Disturbance at Foxwood Court</u>.

Williams, Biddy.

The neighbourhood witch. Lives in Foxwood. Amused by Pip. First appearance: <u>The Disturbance at Foxwood Court</u>.

www.ingramcontent.com/pod-product-compliance
Lightning Source LLC
Chambersburg PA
CBHW032012050726
47590CB00006B/2147